Waiting for Sarah

Waiting for Sarah

BRUCE MCBAY *&* JAMES HENEGHAN

ORCA BOOK PUBLISHERS

National Library of Canada Cataloguing in Publication Data
McBay, Bruce, 1946-

Waiting for Sarah / Bruce McBay, James Heneghan.

ISBN 1-55143-270-6

I. Heneghan, James, 1930- II. Title.

PS8575.B39W34 2003   jC813'.54   C2003-910089-8

PZ7.M1217Wa 2001

First published in the United States, 2003

Library of Congress Control Number: 2002117768

Summary: After Mike loses his family and is severely injured in a car accident, he withdraws until he meets the mysterious Sarah, a girl who is not who she seems.

Orca Book Publishers gratefully acknowledges the support for its publishing programs provided by the following agencies: the Government of Canada through the Book Publishing Industry Development Program (BPIDP), the Canada Council for the Arts, and the British Columbia Arts Council.

Cover design by Christine Toller
Cover photo: jellybeanimages & Robert Youds (top)
Printed and bound in Canada

07 06 05 04 • 6 5 4 3

IN CANADA:
Orca Book Publishers
1030 North Park Street
Victoria, BC Canada
V8T 1C6

IN THE UNITED STATES:
Orca Book Publishers
PO Box 468
Custer, WA   USA
98240-0468

To my mother Christina with love.
BM

For Rebecca.
JH

Our thanks to Tim Sader for his valuable input.

1 . . . last word she ever spoke

In the minute before the crash, the father was squinting into the harsh yellow glare of the late afternoon sun.

The mother, seated beside him, was listening to opera music on the car radio.

In the back seat, behind the mother, the little girl was singing in a high squeal, poking fun at the music.

"Cut it out, Becky," said the mother irritably. "I'm trying to listen. It's the last time I'll tell you."

"Take no notice, Joanne," the driver said. "She's over-excited." He turned his head towards the boy seated behind him, "Calm your sister down, Mike, before she drives us all crazy." But Mike, absorbed in his own thoughts, said nothing.

Becky continued to sing, mimicking the soprano.

Joanne's patience ran out. "Becky!" she yelled.

Her daughter's name was the last word she ever spoke. A truck came at them from the opposite side of the freeway, charging over the grass median and ramming their Chevy head-on with the force of a bomb. In the explosion of metal, plastic and glass, the four occupants were crushed like flies, three of them fatally.

Their deaths were quick.

The lone driver of the runaway truck had been drinking all afternoon. His skull shattered the windshield. His death was also quick.

2 . . . confused and scared

He was confused and scared.

And there was pain. No amount of drugs could take away the pain.

The nurses talked to him, but he understood nothing except he was in a hospital. He tried to ask about his parents and sister, but couldn't understand their replies. He tried to hide in sleep, but always the pain held him, teetering on the edge of consciousness.

After many days, when the pain was almost bearable, the doctor came and explained to him that he was in the Vancouver General Hospital and that they had done their best but had failed to save his legs. Which made no sense because Mike could feel his legs and feet under the covers. They were confusing him with someone else. He asked about his mom and dad and Becky, but their replies made no sense to him. It took another week for him to realize that indeed he had no legs, only bandaged stumps that ended at his knees. Again he asked about his family, and they smiled and nodded.

Later, much later, when he was off the painkillers, when they thought he was strong enough, a doctor and a nurse and a minister gathered about his bed and gently told him that his parents and his little sister had died in the accident.

He was angry.

They tried to console him, but he swore at them and they went away.

After that he was rude to the doctors and nurses and refused to eat and after a while wouldn't speak to anyone, including his two constant visitors, his Aunt Norma and a sixteen-year-old classmate named Robbie. His aunt sat quietly and held his hand whenever she could — when he didn't push her away. Norma and Robbie came every day and talked together in whispers.

He was thin and weak and, because he would not eat, grew even weaker. He was sedated and fed intravenously.

After some weeks, having done all they could for him, the hospital sent him to the rehabilitation center. This would be his home for the next three months, or for as long as it took for him to recover his strength and learn how to walk again with the aid of prosthetics. In the meantime, he would be expected to move about as much as possible in a wheelchair.

But he didn't want to learn how to walk on artificial legs, didn't want a wheelchair, didn't want anything. He threw plates of food at the wall and sometimes at the nurses. In wild tantrums, he yelled and swore at the doctor and nurses and refused to speak with other patients, snarling and snapping at them if they came too close. They soon learned to avoid him. He refused to use a wheelchair or move from his bed. He soiled his bed and clothing rather than ask for bathroom help. His record was marked: *Extrem. Diffic.*

He didn't care. He was alone in his grief. He thought of his parents and Becky and couldn't believe they were gone away from him, disappeared, dead. He could not understand why he had survived; to be alive without them was an agony, a cancer, a fury. He lay on his bed, staring at the ceiling, refusing to speak or eat, ordering his heart to stop beating so his departed family would come to claim him and bear him away.

Aunt Norma and Robbie continued to visit him every day. There were other visitors too — from his school — but he refused to see them.

"You've got to eat, Mike," said Aunt Norma. "I've brought you some bananas and ice-cream; I know you like that."

"And I brought your favorite, Mike," said Robbie, "a Triple-O White Spot burger. You're gonna love it, man."

But he wouldn't eat. His aunt and his friend took the food away.

The Rehab Center staff were patient. They wore him down. Eventually, after two months, he started to speak and eat. He became less difficult, more accepting: He stopped throwing food at the walls and swearing at the nurses; he learned how to move from his bed to a wheelchair and from his wheelchair to his bed, how to wheel himself about, how to take care of himself. But he still kept the world at a distance, growling at everyone, patients, staff and visitors alike, and only occasionally reverting to episodes of anger and self-pity whenever frustrated by his own weakness and physical limitations.

He felt pain in his shins and ankles. "How could that be?" he complained. Dr. Ryan told him that the feeling of pain in his legs was a normal phenomenon.

"But I don't have any damn legs!"

"You know it, Mike, and I know it, but your brain is not yet convinced."

He stared. "But what the ..."

"Relax, it's normal. The common name for it is 'phantom limbs.' As far as your brain is concerned, Mike, your legs are still there. But they're only phantom legs. Sensory ghosts, if you like. It's because of the nerve endings in your thighs. Those nerves supplied your legs. They're not forgotten by your brain. Your brain is sometimes fooled into thinking your legs are still there. You understand?"

"No, I don't understand," he said angrily. "How come I can wiggle my toes?"

"The nerve endings are frayed, like when you cut an electric cable, and they've formed scar tissue, called neuromas. They can be painful. They send impulses — messages — back to the area in your brain that controls toe movements. The same with feelings in other parts of your legs."

"When will the feelings go away?"

"Impossible to say. Some amputees feel nothing. Others experience painful episodes for months, sometimes years. Each case is different."

"Phantom limbs! Hah!" He spat out a swear word, and turned away.

"Wait, Mike!" said Dr. Ryan.

He stopped and swiveled round to face the doctor, a scowl on his face.

"I want to get you fitted for prosthetics. The sooner you start ..."

"Wooden legs? Are you kidding? I'm not interested!"

"Mike. Wait!"

This time he didn't wait, but swore and spun rudely away and wheeled furiously out of the examination room.

He sometimes wheeled himself outside the gates of Rehab to an adjacent park, where he sat out of sight in the greenery and watched the children playing basketball while he shrank into himself like a garden snail.

3 . . . a pointless waste of time

Leaving the Rehab Center was not hard: he hated the place. From now on he would live with his Aunt Norma.

Norma McCleod lived alone at the Leinster Housing Co-operative at False Creek. Because of Mike, and co-op by-laws, she had recently exchanged her one-bedroom unit for one with two bedrooms, on the third, and top, floor. The rooms were small and, like many other new buildings in Vancouver, the Leinster Co-op was having problems with leaks. As well, third-floor residents complained of constant and unpleasant curry odors. On the positive side, the building was close to shopping and the city center. Norma worried that Mike might not like the place and, never having had the responsibility of looking after another person, also worried whether she would be able to cope with her nephew's black moods and physical limitations. She knew she was taking on a lot. Would she be up to the job? That was her greatest fear. A physiotherapist and a counselor and other experts from the Rehab Center, and people from the Ministry of Human Resources, had visited the co-op, asking Norma the same kinds of questions, bringing her books and pamphlets and suggesting changes to the apartment. They advised her to join a support group at the center. Carpenters and builders came and widened doorways for the wheelchair — the entrance to the apartment, the bathroom and Mike's room. They also installed two automatic pocket doors, lowered a section of kitchen counter, lowered kitchen cupboards and installed other special equipment such as handrails in the bathroom. Carpeting was removed to make way for wood floors.

Her misgivings were confirmed almost right away. Though Mike seemed not to mind his small room, once installed, he refused to leave the building.

"But you've got to go out, Mike. The fresh air and exercise will do you good."

"No, it won't."

"And you must start thinking of going back to school."

"I don't want to go back to school."

Norma was dismayed. "But you've got to go back."

"No, I don't."

"But Mike, what about graduation?" his aunt pleaded.

"I don't care about graduation."

That was all he would say.

Early one morning there was a knock on the door. Norma had just left for work.

"Who is it?" he asked through the closed door.

"District Services for Mike Scott. My name's Taylor."

"What do you want?" he shouted back.

"Could you open the door?"

He opened the door. A dark man, flat face, black hair and eyebrows, long olive-green raincoat, heavy briefcase, showed his ID. "I'm the district teacher for the home-bound, Mike." He smiled. "I'd like to talk to you about school assignments."

"Don't need any assignments."

"Could I come in so we can talk?" He took half a step forward.

"No!" Mike slammed the door and the man went away.

He came back the next day. "It's Mr. Taylor," he said through the closed door. "I have to talk to you, Mike."

"Drop dead!"

"Open this door!" Mr. Taylor said firmly.

Mike told him to go away in language that curled the paint off the door.

Mr. Taylor left.

He told Norma that evening. "Makes no sense," he said. "Who cares about school? Who cares about graduating? It's all such a pointless waste of time."

Norma didn't argue, but left him alone with his thoughts. She went out to work, cooked his meals, cleaned his room of sour smells and dust and did his laundry. In the evenings when she got home from work she invariably found him in his wheelchair at the window, staring out at the city towers and the North Shore mountains.

4 . . . waiting forever

He stares out the window at the city towers and North
Shore mountains, remembering his mother, who is
standing and smiling, eyes closed, face raised to the
sun. Birds come to her and flock about her and alight
on her hands and shoulders and brush her face with
their wings. It is only an image, one he has dreamed
up probably, but it seems true all the same.

He remembers her as she was on the day of the
accident. His father and Becky are still upstairs. It is
very early in the morning. Birds sing in the trees and
gardens. His mother wears her blue track suit —
the one Dad got her for Christmas. Already she has
been out for her daily run along the sea wall and is
now working in the kitchen, peeling and chopping,
preparing food so their supper will be ready when
they get back home from the annual air show. It is
to be a curried carrot-parsnip soup and lentil sambar.
His mother enjoys cooking. Mike can see the recipe
names in her cookbook spread out in front of her
on the counter, its pages marked with more than a
dozen yellow Post-It notes. The radio plays music.

As she works, she frequently looks out the window at the birds in her patio feeder — mostly finches in the summer, sparrows and starlings in the winter. Because of the music she hasn't heard him, doesn't know he is behind her, leaning in the doorway, stealing some of her pleasure as she gathers up the bright promise of the August morning with the work and smell of the food and the sight and sounds of the birds.

His thoughts leap ahead to the day's end, when they are driving home from the Abbotsford Air Show, and then the accident and the three of them dead, and he thinks of the soup and the lentils in their pots, waiting forever, as the empty house grows dark and the birds stop their singing.

5 . . . a wonderful future

There were support services, from Rehab mainly, counselors and therapists of various kinds. Like the visiting teacher, they came, but Mike refused to open the door to them. He told them to go away. The visiting teacher came again, but by now Mike wasn't answering the door or the telephone; he was closing his bedroom door and keeping his silence, pretending he was out.

Occasionally he stayed in bed all day, doing nothing, and Norma would come home to find him curled up in a fetal position under the covers, or lying — still in his pajamas — with his hands behind his head, staring at the ceiling. He had very little to say, never asking his aunt how she was or how her workday had gone, nothing. He had no interest in anybody or anything.

The walls of the apartment were becoming badly marked with scuffs and scrapes from the wheelchair and he was forever dropping glasses and plates. Norma pretended not to notice; according to the therapists it was all a part of Mike's adjustment.

He continued in this way for several months. When Norma's friends came to the apartment for coffee and gossip Mike went to his room and closed the door. Sometimes Norma visited with other residents of the building, leaving a telephone number for Mike in case he needed her. He never did, even though he usually fell once or twice a day, in the bathroom usually, or sometimes from his wheelchair in the kitchen as he reached up to cupboards or shelves, then rescued himself with loud and angry curses.

She surprised him one evening by inviting a friend, a pastor from the church. Mike knew what she was up to all right; this was obviously his aunt's attempt to smuggle in a dose of spiritual guidance. The pastor's name was Samuel Butterworth, and he tried to get Mike to talk about himself and the accident. He had silver-gray hair, wore small, round glasses and had the kind of twinkling blue eyes that invited confidences. Mike refused to talk to him, turning his back rudely and wheeling away to his room.

Another evening Norma invited the woman from across the hall for herb tea. Mrs. Dhaliwal — Norma called her Dolly — had been Norma's friend for many years, ever since (Norma later explained to Mike) it had fallen to Norma to deal with co-op neighbors' complaints against the Dhaliwal family concerning the strong smell of curry on the third floor.

Dolly Dhaliwal was short and plump and wore a bright flowing sari, mostly green and red, and brought with her not only the herb tea and a plate of sticky cakes but also a painted wooden box containing cards, dice, coins, incense, tiny bottles of oils, medallions, glass pyramids and other esoteric articles, all with the intention of foretelling Norma's future.

Mike, attracted to the cakes like a wasp to jam, stayed for tea. The aroma of the tea caused the apartment to smell like an eastern temple. Dolly began, not with Norma, but with Mike, surprising him by grasping his right palm, raising it to within a few inches of her sharp brown nose and staring down into it for several seconds. Then she said, "You have a yellow and green aura about you; lines here are full of joy. I see a wonderful future for you. Someone will come and bring you great happiness. You will see. It will be soon."

Mike didn't believe in clairvoyance or prophecy or any of Mrs. Dhaliwal's arts. It was all rubbish as far as he was concerned. "Thanks for the valuable information, Mrs. Dhaliwal," he said, not bothering to conceal the sneer in his voice. "It's good to know what a wonderful future I've got coming." He took the last cake from the plate on the table and went off to his room.

Later, after Mrs. Dhaliwal had gone, Norma was angry. "You were not very polite."

"I don't believe all that fortune-telling stuff; it's stupid."

"It's just for fun. There's no harm in it."

"It's phony. Except for the cakes; they were okay."

"You took too many."

He shrugged. "So what. Lighten up."

"You don't have to be so discourteous to my friends, Mike. That's all I'll say. The matter's now closed."

"How did you solve the problem of the curry smell?"

"Dolly solved it herself, by baking delicious little treats for the entire third floor — samosas and gulab jamans. There isn't one person who can resist them. Once people got to know Dolly and like her, well, the problem was solved."

Norma drove him out to the Burnaby cemetery so he could see the grave. The day was cold and crisp under a blue sky. She pushed him along the path between the headstones. A thin layer of frost on the grass had started to melt. He helped push his chair onto the grass. Norma had brought flowers, chrysanthemums, which she placed on the grave, removing those withered by frost.

He stared at the granite stone and the names of his family: "Died August 15, 1998." His eyes stung.

"It was a lovely funeral," said Norma. "The Reverend Butterworth read the eulogy. So nice. Everyone was there — Robbie, the kids from Carleton High and Sanderson Elementary — looked to me like every kid in the neighborhood turned out — and teachers, and people from the school board. 'Tell Mike to hang in there,' they said. You were in people's minds. It was like you were there with us, Mike."

He said nothing, thinking. Then he said, "How come if there were so many kids at the funeral none of them came to see me in the hospital?"

Norma was surprised. "But they did! You were always sleeping, or perhaps you don't remember because of the painkillers. The nurses allowed only two people at one time and had to send many of them away. You sent many of them away yourself. Do you remember?"

He shook his head, then thought for a while longer and said, "So there was a big crowd at the funeral?"

"Enormous. There were women from MADD — Mothers Against Drunk Driving. A very sincere group of women, I'm sure, but to tell you the truth I could have done without the TV cameras."

On the drive home Norma wondered aloud why he had never asked about his home, their three-bedroom townhouse on Fairview Slopes, the one they had moved into when Mike was only five, the place where Becky was born.

"Who cares about a house!"

"It was your home, Mike. Anyway, there were mortgage payments. So I arranged for it to be sold. You should know that there's a small equity from the sale and a small amount from insurance. It's in trust for when you reach eighteen."

He shrugged. He didn't care about the money.

"And I had a few things put in storage. One or two pieces of furniture Joanne was fond of. And your father's stuff — golf clubs, medals, his computer hardware; it's all there if you ever decide to use it. I couldn't deal with it, so just had everything boxed and stored. You might feel like going through it after a little time has passed. I kept some things from your room separate — your posters and CDs, things like that; they're stored in my locker in the co-op basement if you decide you want them."

He said nothing; he was thinking of gravestones.

6 . . . there are no answers

He really did care about his home, sold now, which meant that everything was gone. His whole life was gone, like a torpedoed ship at the bottom of the sea, leaving him a lone survivor in an empty ocean with nothing to cling to — except for Norma and Robbie. Dolly Dhaliwal and her "wonderful future" indeed!

He remembered his room. And Becky's. And downstairs, the worn living-room carpeting and shabby sofa his mother talked about replacing, but never did. The family eating together in the evenings. Rules and arguments about behavior and chores and the Internet and TV watching. Ordinary lives that were meant to go on in an ordinary way for many years, but were now just memories.

"Why is this building so damn noisy?" he asked Norma one afternoon.

Norma pulled a face. "It's the workmen mending leaks in the building. You must have noticed the blue tarps around the outside. They shouldn't be here more than a month or so."

The din of hammers, saws and drills seemed

louder in the second week. "I hate this place," he said.

Norma hid her hurt feelings. "The work will soon be finished."

"Why have you got leaks? Why is it taking so long? What's the matter with this damn place any-way?" He noticed his aunt flinch, but didn't care.

"Moisture gets through the siding and rots the drywall. We sued the developer. It has taken two whole years to make them do repairs." Norma watched Mike's face as she explained. It was the first interest he had shown in anything in a long time — a negative interest, but a positive sign, she reckoned.

One evening after supper, when she noticed him staring trance-like at the pattern in the tablecloth, she said, "Don't be so hard on yourself, Mike."

He looked at her. "What do you mean?"

"I know how much you miss your parents and Becky. But the accident was just that: an accident. None of it was your fault."

"Yes, but ..." He shook his head. His eyes glistened with angry tears. "Why should they be gone, while I ...?"

She grasped his hands. "Sometimes there are no answers, Mike. Life is like that: a puzzle. But God has reasons for everything, even if we don't understand. Your mother and I were very close, almost like twins. I miss her very much also, and Becky and your father. You are Joanne's son and you're a fine brave boy, Mike. But your mom and dad and Becky are no longer here with us. You've got to let them go."

He shook his head and wheeled away to his room.

7 . . . time to start living

He started going out alone, away from the constant noise of the builders. The din made him angry; there was no peace. He pushed his wheelchair along the hallway, around and over the obstacle course of the contractor's equipment, and took the elevator down from the third floor, where he had to maneuver his chair around ladders, building materials, ropes and tarps in the entrance lobby. Then he wheeled himself along the sea wall to the marina at Stamps Landing. It was quiet there, with only the tinkling conversations of bells on sailboat masts breaking the silence. He sat and watched the lazy activity in the marina and the silent boat traffic in False Creek, which isn't a creek at all but an inlet from the sea. But even here he found no peace.

Weekends, Norma offered to push him all the way to the Granville Island Market, but his friend Robbie took over that job instead. Mike enjoyed his outings with Robbie.

Norma brought up the subject of the support

services. "You must be reasonable, Mike. Your therapy wasn't finished when you left Rehab; there's still much that can be done. Dr. Ryan says you should have prosthet — "

"Ryan's a jerk. I don't need anybody poking at me and asking questions."

"Mike, Rehab calls me at work. They're worried about you. As well as Dr. Ryan there's a physiotherapist named Finch, and a man named Taylor from the School Board who complains that you won't open the door. What am I supposed to do?"

"Tell 'em to go to — "

"Well, if you won't listen to Rehab at least you're well enough to go back to school," Norma interrupted firmly. "You can't mope about like this, doing nothing, staring out the window or sitting on the sea wall watching the boats all day."

"I don't want to go back to school."

"You've got to go. Your mother wouldn't like it if you didn't. Joanne wouldn't want me to sit idly by and watch you become an under-educated, anti-social hermit. I won't allow it. It's time to start living again, Mike. School is the perfect place to begin."

"I hate school."

"Your mother told me you liked school. You were a good student."

"What can I do … in this?" he burst out angrily.

"Many people have wheelchairs, Mike. They manage. They cope. They get on with their lives. You still have your good mind. And your arms and shoulders. There are many worse off than you."

"Worse off! You mean like *no* arms as well as *no*

legs and *no* family? Hah!" He was in a furious temper.

"You could get rid of the wheelchair and walk if you wanted. Dr. Ryan says ... "

But he wasn't listening. He was too angry. Norma was beginning to think she'd moved too soon; he wasn't ready yet to join the world. But she couldn't go back now.

"Mike! You've just got to stop beating up on yourself." She pulled over a chair and sat facing him. "Your mother is gone," she said firmly. "And your dad. And Becky. And there's *nothing* anyone can do to bring them back. One thing I do know and it's this: they would want you to be happy. You're here and you're alive. And they would want you to go to school. Once you're back you'll find everyone is on your side ..."

"Forget it!" Without another word, he spun his wheelchair, rudely turning his back on his aunt, and pushed himself angrily away.

The weeks and months went by. By now he had missed the whole of grade eleven. With the next school year approaching, one year after the accident that had claimed the lives of his family, his aunt became persistent. And so did Robbie.

"Give it a try, Mike, okay?" said Robbie. "The kids at Carleton are pretty good. They're gonna be on your side. They'll be real happy to see you back, man, honest!"

Finally he gave in. Boredom temporarily overcame fear and bitterness; that was the reason. Another reason was the offer of credit for the missed year. Unusual and extenuating circumstances, the school called it, which meant he could, if he wished, stay with his class, pick up a few of the missed grade eleven units and graduate on schedule. That was the clincher. Not that he cared about graduating — he cared about nothing — but his Aunt Norma cared. Except for Robbie she was the only one who did care. Robbie and Norma had stuck with him, visiting hospital and Rehab every day, even when he'd given them the silent treatment, even when he'd yelled and sworn at them, even when he'd thrown their gifts to the floor; he owed it to his aunt. She was a true friend, not like some of the so-called friends of his dead parents who had made one visit or had sent one Get Well card and then nothing. A few of the other family friends had continued to visit and bring gifts but soon stopped when he had nothing to say to them. It had been much easier to feign sleep when visitors came. Aunt Norma, on the other hand, had turned out to be a source of strength. She was really something else. And so was Robbie. He didn't know what he would have done without them.

8 . . . despised them all

He returned reluctantly to Carleton High in September, over a year since his accident. He did it only to please his aunt.

He was alone. Robbie had wanted to be there, but Mike said no; he had to do it by himself. Full of purpose, he pushed his chair towards the main entrance. But then he stopped. There were steps. He'd forgotten about the steps. How was he going to get up that formidable obstacle and in the front door? He looked up at the school motto above the entrance as if the answer he needed was to be found there: *ad summum*, "To the Heights." The building was old and lacking ramps. He looked at the steps again. There was no way he could get his chair up to the entrance. Annoyance turned to anger. Damned school! Was there a way around the back?

"You take one side and I'll take the other."

It was Robbie with another boy and they were grasping his chair and carrying him up the steps. Mike kept his eyes closed until they had put him down in the front hall. Then he glared at his friend.

"I told you I'd manage by my — "

Robbie turned away. "Thanks," he said to his helper.

The boy smiled. "No problem," he said as he walked away.

Robbie turned back to Mike and grinned. "There's an entrance around the back. It's near the band room. No steps. I knew you wouldn't remember." He turned on his heel before Mike could say anything else. "See you later. If you're polite maybe I'll walk home with you." He grinned again and was gone.

Mike looked around. It seemed to him that every eye was on him. He wheeled past the band room and through the halls, staring straight ahead, scowling, hating everyone. The secretary in the school office had his timetable ready. He snatched it from her hand and turned to go.

She stopped him with a word. "Wait."

He paused, but did not look back.

"Mr. Warren, the vice-principal, wants to see you before you …"

"Well, I don't want to see him."

He found his first class and insisted on sitting at the back of the room. Desks were moved; space was made for him. If anyone stared he glared back at them, and they turned away, withered by his hate.

Even Carleton's new, cute and over-excited eighth graders, all with two strong legs, all with mothers and fathers and brothers and sisters, all with proper homes and families. He despised them all.

3 . . . back with friends

Robbie helped him home, pushing on the uphill parts.

"So how was it, Mike? How did it go?"

He played dumb. "How did what go?"

"You know. Classes, crowded hallways, being back with friends, stuff like that."

"Friends! Hmmph!" He was still ticked off at Robbie for lifting him up the school steps. He'd felt so helpless. "Who was that other kid this morning?"

"What other kid are you talking about, man?" Robbie playing the innocent.

"I'm talking about the one who helped with the skyride."

"Oh, him. He's a new guy. In my history class. He's big and he happened to be passing by so I grabbed him. Name's Ben Packard."

"Hmmph!"

He went to school every day.

He hated it.

He was unfriendly. Kids he'd known for years,

who had been with him through elementary school, he ignored as though they were strangers; he wanted nobody's sympathy. He was asked to join the year-book committee. "Not interested," he told them. He was invited to join the chess club and the debating club, but he refused; he was no longer interested in chess, and as for debating, he didn't much like the sponsor teacher, Mr. Dorfman. So he joined no clubs. Mr. Estereicher, a popular PE teacher, asked him if he might be interested in wheelchair sports; there was a meet coming up, and Estereicher would be happy to coach him for track or basketball or whatever interested him. "I don't give a damn about wheelchair sports — thanks very much," he added sarcastically.

People soon learned to leave him alone.

They didn't like him. He didn't care.

Someone hung a bumper-sticker on the back of his wheelchair: Ban Leg-hold Traps. Robbie managed to remove it without Mike knowing.

10 . . . fright mask

By the end of October it was almost as though he had never been away from Carleton High. The school was still the same, but he had changed. In tenth grade he had been busily involved in the school's classes and activities; now everything was meaningless. He endured it only because of Aunt Norma and Robbie.

Today he had Dorfman first period. He didn't like Dorfman's class. He didn't like Dorfman. History should be interesting, exciting even, but Dorfman managed to convert it into sleeping pills. For the first fifteen minutes of each seventy-five minute period there was a quiz on yesterday's notes. If you forgot to memorize the notes you lost the fifteen marks. When the quiz was over it was note-taking from the overhead projector for tomorrow's quiz. Notes and quizzes, always notes, one mind-numbing page after another. In addition to all this, Dorfman expected him to hand in two lengthy essays on eleventh grade topics, ones he had missed.

Dorfman stood at the front of the room, behind his overhead projector, the classroom lights out. Except for the windows, most of the light came from the projector's 300 watts of non-enlightenment thrown onto the wall-screen behind and over Dorfman's glittering baldness, poorly covered by a phony comb-over. Whenever Dorfman leaned into the projector to operate the roller, the light reflected off his thick-lensed glasses, hiding his usually magnified eyes and shining up under his face, accentuating the thick wet lips and flat nose, twisting his features into a Halloween fright mask.

Mike sat at the back near the window. He'd had Dorfman before, in tenth grade, and used to copy his notes religiously, never missing a word. Now he didn't care about taking notes. Instead, he simply scanned them idly as they came up on the screen, and then went back to his book, *The History of Flight*, always handy in his packsack slung behind his wheelchair, glancing up again only when he heard the squeak of the rollers.

In his first class, when Dorfman had caught him reading his book instead of furiously scribbling history notes like the other kids, he'd threatened to have him expelled. Mike had shrugged. "So expel me."

Dorfman had stared at him angrily through lenses like the bottoms of pop bottles. No more was said about expulsion. Besides, Mike always managed to pass the daily quiz. And he was in a wheelchair; what kind of teacher would expel a kid in a wheelchair?

11 . . . the dead are everywhere

Robbie's two small cousins were visiting for Halloween and Robbie had agreed to take them on a trick-or-treat tour of his neighborhood. "Why don't you join us?" he said to Mike. "Should be fun. Jimmy and Sharon are going as aliens, so I'm gonna join them in a Boba Fett bounty hunter mask."

"No, thanks. I'm too old for that stuff."

"You don't have to dress up. Just come as you are."

"Meaning what? I look like a natural freak?"

"Aw, come on, Mike. You always liked Halloween, remember?"

"How old are your cousins?"

"Jimmy's eight, Sharon's six."

In the end he agreed to go. Robbie was like a little kid, eager and excited over the smallest thing, like wearing a mask and shepherding his little cousins around. It was the least Mike could do; Robbie was always there when Mike needed him. Easygoing and good-natured, he never expected anything in return.

The weather cooperated. The day had been

sunny and cold. In the late afternoon a mist had descended, making it the perfect evening for a haunting. Robbie wore his Boba Fett mask just as he had threatened, and his excited young cousins were dressed as Martians.

"This time last year you were in Rehab," said Robbie.

He didn't answer. He was looking at Jimmy and Sharon, so thrilled to be out in the dark, and thinking of Becky who would be eleven if she ...

He thought about his dad and his own feelings of — what? Inadequacy? Inferiority? How he'd never seemed to please his father, not that his dad ever complained or criticized. It didn't seem to matter whether it was school grades or basketball or track, nothing Mike ever did drew praise from his dad. "Running is okay," he would say to his son. "And basketball's okay too. But the bike is where it's really at." Will Scott had been a competitive cyclist when he was young, and had plenty of racing medals to show for it. Mike knew that his dad wished he would take up cycling, but he simply wasn't interested. Maybe it was his dad persuading him to watch all those boring Tour de France stages on television when he was a little kid that turned him against it; he didn't know, but he was darned if he was going to take up a sport he didn't even like and none of his friends was interested in.

And now it was too late: he would never hear from his dad those few words he had always wanted, those words that said simply ...

"Trick or treat!" Jimmy and Sharon squealing at an opening door brought him back to the present.

Jimmy and Sharon wanted to help push Mike's chair. "Sure," said Mike.

Robbie said, "You know what, Mike?"

"What?"

"Tonight is the first time in a year you haven't growled at everyone. Must be the Halloween spirit."

Mike shrugged. Halloween this year seemed different. Strange. As though there really *were* ghosts in the air. He could feel them. The dead are everywhere, he thought, surrounding him in the darkness and in the misty lamplight. He could feel them in the streets and in the trees and in the garden hedges, hovering at the edge of visibility.

Maybe Mom and Dad and Becky were out there too, watching over him; he refused to accept that they were gone forever, that he would never see them again. They had been together, one family, noisy and alive, and now they were gone. He'd never realized that life hung on such a thin, weak thread, that death could so easily snap it, that your normal, everyday life and routines, and your home, could change so drastically that you weren't the same person anymore.

The mist swirled under yellow streetlights.

Mom and Dad and Becky, buried under a granite stone at Forest Lawn Cemetery. But their spirits were out there somewhere, in the misty darkness.

In a better place.

He had to believe it.

It was Halloween. Robbie was showing off for his cousins and having fun.

Witches and goblins and ghosts took over the neighborhood.

12 . . . didn't need anyone

Lunch-time in the noisy cafeteria. He ignored the kids around him and read his book. Robbie was late.

"Can I get you anything?"

He looked up. It was the big lunk who had helped Robbie manhandle his chair into the school in September — what was his name, Bill Packard? He was new at Carleton; that was all Robbie had said about him. No, not Bill — Ben. That was it — Ben Packard.

"No," Mike growled.

"I'm on my way to the pop machine. Thought you might need a Coke or something."

"I said no."

Packard smiled. "It's my treat."

Mike swiveled his chair so that his back was to the boy. Idiot; couldn't he understand plain English? Couldn't he see he was busy reading? He went back to his book.

"Please yourself," said Packard, shrugging and walking away.

After he had eaten his lunch there was still no sign of Robbie, so he aimed his wheelchair towards the exit, skillfully avoiding kids, chairs and table edges. As he reached the door his way was blocked by a girl with glasses. Margaret Cowley.

"Mike Scott!" she yelled. "The very man I'm looking for."

Scowling, he tried to swerve around and past her, but she danced backwards and blocked his way once more.

"Mike! Stop! This is *important*!"

He hated it when people came too close to his chair and leaned down and bellowed at him, like just because he had no legs he was, what — deaf and stupid? Margaret Cowley's loud voice made him back away.

But she followed. "It's the millennium, Mike. It's also Carleton's fiftieth ... "

He backed off some more. And just in case she hadn't got the message he growled, "Get out of my face."

That did it: she stood still but continued talking. "... Carleton's fiftieth anniversary this year, Mike, as you already know, I'm sure."

He said nothing, the scowl still on his face. The scowl was one he had practiced in the mirror. It was ugly. It was meant to keep people away.

But not Cowley. "So we're putting out a special millennium golden jubilee edition of the school yearbook. I'm editor-in-chief. The alumni association and student council are shelling out extra funding." She flashed him a bright, triumphant smile.

He glared at her.

"I know you said you're not interested in the yearbook committee, but we need your help, Mike; the alumni association needs your help, the student council needs your help, Carleton High needs your help, and … " She fixed him with a bright owlish stare. "… I need your help."

"I'm busy."

"But history is your thing. You're good at it. You get As off old Dorfman, which is the same as winning gold medals at the Olymp — "

"Not any more, I don't."

"Well you used to. Anyway, *we*, the committee want you — you were top choice — to write a history of Carleton High for us. For the yearbook. For posterity. For the millennium!"

He started to move away, but she followed him.

"We need you, Mike. It needn't be long. A few thousand words. With pictures if you can find any. Your name will be on it, of course: Mike Scott, author. What do you say?"

Cowley's voice was loud even for the noisy cafeteria. He swiveled his chair away, turning his back on her, starting to flee, but in his haste bumped the table ahead of him. A pop bottle crashed to the floor. He didn't apologize. His lunch bag, empty except for a banana peel, slipped off his lap onto the floor. He ignored it, trying to extricate his chair and escape from Margaret Cowley. Cowley picked up Mike's lunch bag. Then she picked up the boy's bottle, still in one piece, replaced it on the table and handed Mike his brown paper lunch bag. "What do you say, Mike? Will you help us out?"

"No." He started towards the exit once again.

She danced ahead and blocked his way. "I can try and get you out of Dorfman's class for as long as it takes to do the job." Her earnest face took on a smug look with this demonstration of her power and importance.

He stopped. Getting out of Dorfman's history class was about as easy as breaking out of Alcatraz.

Cowley almost fell over the wheelchair when it stopped so suddenly. But she could see him hesitate, and pounced. "Agree to work on Carleton's history, Mike, and I'll do my best to spring you from Dorfman's class. What do you say?"

He didn't really need to consider the question. It would be trading seventy-five minutes of boredom for hanging out in the library every day. He would never admit it to Cowley, but he used to enjoy poring over old magazines and newspapers and files and pictures — the real stuff of history, not mind-numbing pages of notes from an overhead. He suddenly felt enthusiastic about Carleton's golden jubilee, but pretended to consider the question, frowning and rubbing his chin, not wanting Cowley to see how pleased he was or to think she was doing him any favors. "Hmm," he mumbled. He glanced around. Most of the kids, lunches finished, had wandered out into the late November fog. He could see over Cowley's shoulder that Robbie was coming their way, carrying a bag of French fries. If Mike were a painter, which he was not, and he had the job of painting a portrait of Robbie, it would show him nursing a bag of fries close to his more-than-plump middle while he pushed a fistful into his round, happy face.

He returned his scowl to Cowley's hopeful face.

"Well, Mike?" she said. "Will you go along with the project? For the school?"

"Okay," he said flatly. "I'll do it. But only if you get me out of Dorfman's class."

She smiled.

"For the rest of the semester."

Her smile disappeared. "I'm not so sure …"

"I also want a guaranteed pass for his cruddy course."

"Oh!" Her face fell. "That might be stretching things a bit."

"Them's the conditions."

"I don't think he'll go for it. But I'll try. If I try really hard for the pass and I don't get it, but I *do* get the time-out, will you do it for me anyway?"

"No."

He didn't care that much about passing Dorfman's stupid course, or about any of his other courses either, but he knew he had a few class marks, enough when combined with provincial exam marks, to get him through. That should satisfy his aunt.

Cowley was still babbling. "… I've already talked to Miss Pringle — she's the yearbook sponsor again this year — and she's arranging for the library archives to be opened up for whoever takes the job. I told her it'd probably be you."

He stared into the glint of her glasses. "I didn't know we had archives at Carleton."

Robbie parked himself on the table top next to Mike, stuffing fries into his smile.

Cowley pulled out a chair from under the table

and sat down. Now she and Mike were on the same level. "It's a little room off the library," she said. "Nobody ever goes in. It's kept locked. The key is in Pringle's office on a hook behind the door. She let me take a quick look inside." She pulled a face. "It's a bit of a mess, but you'd be left alone in there. Be your own boss; no Dorfman, no overhead notes ..."

Mike, already enjoying the picture of himself up to his ears in old historical documents and photographs, let her ramble on; he was only half listening, thinking how he would do almost anything to be away from his history teacher: the man depressed him.

His attention returned to Cowley.

"... she could help you sort out the chaos a bit, help you find stuff ..."

"Who?"

"The *girl*."

"What girl?"

Cowley gave a sigh. "The eighth grade kid from the yearbook committee I just finished telling you about. As I said, we've got plenty of eager beavers on the committee this year. Do you want a girl?"

Robbie butted in. "I want her. Especially if she's cute."

Cowley glared at him. "You should watch that waistline, Robbie. It's already bigger than your IQ."

Robbie blinked.

"You're a cow, Cowley," Mike growled. "And you're not exactly anorexic yourself."

"Thanks," said Cowley, unruffled. "What about the girl?"

"I prefer to work alone." He didn't need a girl, didn't need anyone. It would be good to be alone in Carleton's archives, looking through old year-books.

"What was all that about, man?" asked Robbie when Margaret Cowley had gone.

Mike explained.

"Sounds as bad as Dorfman's class to me, though come to think of it, maybe you could catch up on your sleep. Want some fries? Where are the archives anyway?"

Mike declined the out-thrust bag with a shake of his head. "There's a small locked room, back of the library. Cowley says nobody ever goes in there, not even Pringle. Think of all those old school newspapers stashed away, and yearbooks and photos and who-knows-what-else."

"Cobwebs maybe," said Robbie. "And ghosts." He laughed.

Mike noticed his friend's laugh was a bit strained. Cowley's insult had hit home. He knew Robbie was sensitive about his weight. Some of the other kids made fun of him behind his back, calling him names. Overweight people (people of weight?) were discriminated against as much as "people of color." Robbie was also sensitive about his low grades. There were only two things Robbie didn't like: exercise and schoolwork. It wasn't that he was lazy or dumb or anything; he had a sharp intelligence and a terrific memory, especially for anything to do with the movies, even the old ones that went way back to before he was born, back even to when films had no sound. But that was all he ever read: books about movies and the history of movies, famous directors, film star biographies — certainly not school texts.

Mike gave Robbie's knee an understanding slap. "Take no notice of Cowley. She doesn't have your great personality, Robbie. Forget her."

Robbie's big face broke into a happy smile. He offered his bag again. "One left. Just for you."

"Thanks."

Robbie bounced up, grasped the handles of the wheelchair and whirled Mike expertly through the hallways and out into Vancouver's fog and damp.

13 . . . lord of the files

The archives room was small and smelled musty.

Today was Thursday. Margaret Cowley had been quick getting to his history teacher. She hadn't managed to extract a promise of a pass for the course, but Dorfman seemed willing to help the yearbook committee — or to seize the opportunity of ridding himself of Mike's disturbing presence in his classroom.

He summoned Mike to appear before him after school. The classroom was empty and the overworked overhead projector was off, though its cooling fan still whirred furiously. "If you produce a substantial history of Carleton High, Scott," he said — pale eyes staring from behind thick lenses — "then a pass will be considered. Produce a masterpiece," — wet lips widening in a sarcastic grin — "and earn an A. Do you understand?"

Mike nodded. What a jerk.

"I expect you to demonstrate how well you can work with primary source materials — newspapers and yearbooks mainly — and whatever else your research skills might provide. Remember, you have already missed a year of school, so you will need to work extremely hard if you hope to pass the course."

Moron.

Come to think of it, Mike hated all the teachers. And the students. And he hated Carleton High, and didn't give a damn for their stupid golden jubilee fiftieth anniversary, or whatever Cowley said it was.

Which was why working alone in the archives during the history period appealed to him so much; he would be away from Dorfman and the other kids; he wouldn't have to put up with their sidelong looks, their smiles of sympathy; he wanted nothing to do with any of them.

He surveyed the archives room. A single, bare electric bulb hung from a cobwebbed cord in the center of the ceiling. High up on the end wall opposite the door a small window grudgingly allowed the morning sun to elbow its way through a filter of grime and cobwebs. Under the window there was a wash basin, its taps corroded and green. A rectangular table stood in the middle of the room underneath the light, its wooden top heaped with bundles of dusty papers. A plain wooden chair and stool completed the furniture. The rest of the room consisted of shelving, eight feet high on all four walls, each shelf crammed full with file boxes, school yearbooks and untidy bundles of *Clarion*s representing fifty years of Carleton's journalism classes.

He started by clearing the table of its junk, heaping papers and boxes on the floor against a bank of shelves, planning to examine it all later after he'd made a work station for himself. The room needed a thorough vacuuming. With hands and forearms he swept the dust off the table top, revealing dark mahogany scarred with old initials. He ran his fingers over the carved initials, wondering about their owners, who they were and what had become of them. Then he sat back in his wheelchair, shirt and cut-off jeans — ends sewn thigh length so nobody had to see his white, mutilated knees — already covered in dust, hands on the tabletop. This would be his workbench, his center of operations. History was about to be made here. He was Mike Scott, Lord of the Files, King of the Archives, supreme ruler of all he surveyed.

Raising himself up on the arms of his wheelchair to gain a better view of the higher shelves, he reckoned there were about fifty bundles of *Clarion* newspapers, each tied around the middle with twine. Probably one bundle for each year. Many of the bundles had burst open, so that clumps of separated newspapers lay scattered untidily about the floor.

The yearbooks hadn't been organized, at least he couldn't see anywhere a neat row of forty-nine editions, each one a different color. Instead, there were yearbooks everywhere, in various dusty colors — green, blue, even pink — many of them duplicate copies: piled on the floor, crammed in between newspaper bundles, stacked under and over and around file boxes, or lying where they had fallen onto the floor with the fugitive newspapers.

He felt like Lord Carnarvon opening up the three-thousand-year-old tomb of King Tutankhamen and feasting his eyes on its glittering treasures for the first time.

To work. He wheeled over to the wall where he

could see eight or nine books with identical red covers, duplicates obviously, stacked on one easy-to-reach shelf. He grasped the top copy, blew the dust off, and saw the date: 1971. He peered up at the higher shelves. How would he get up there? He should have thought of that, should have agreed to let Cowley supply one of her little eighth grade shin-kickers, even if it was only for ten or fifteen minutes each period, someone who could climb up on the stool to the high places, who could help him organize this dusty tomb. He had to admit it: his bad temper didn't always get him what he wanted. "Yes, Margaret, I'd appreciate the help," might have been the smart response.

But he had looked forward to working alone. He could have asked for a boy, but boys steered clear of committees, everyone knew that; the yearbook committee was usually a girl thing. But a young girl would be a disaster. Young girls chattered. How would he get any work done with a chattering girl? And eighth-grade girls giggled; everyone knew how much they giggled; eighth-grade girls hardly ever stopped chattering and giggling; that was what eighth-grade girls mainly did; they chattered and giggled. And worse, they were always asking questions and wanting to take over and boss you around. An eighth-grade girl was a no-no; an eighth-grade girl was definitely out.

Except Becky. Becky chattered all the time, but she was different; hers was interesting chatter; he wouldn't have minded that, not at all. Besides, she was only ten, and had opinions on almost everything, like cloning, for example: "Boys are unnecessary.

They're selfish and rude and stupid. I won't ever get married; I'll clone my daughter, and when she grows up she can do the same and that way I'll never ever die." And she asked stupid questions that made him laugh.

Used to make him laugh. Before the accident. Before she was squashed to death like a summer bug on a windshield.

His thoughts were black. Think of something else.

Maybe Robbie could help get the stuff off the high shelves!

Except there might be a problem getting him out of class. Could the powerful editor-in-chief Cowley arrange that too? If she convinced Dorfman she could convince anybody. He would ask her today. Robbie would be perfect: he didn't chatter, didn't giggle, didn't make silly suggestions, didn't try to take over and boss you around, and was the best pal a guy could ever have.

Meanwhile, to work. Make a start. He pulled out a file box and blew off the dust before letting it fall into his lap. It was heavy. He wheeled over and lifted the box up onto the table and suddenly felt closed in, trapped in his wheelchair and a prisoner in the dimly lighted room. He felt the shortage of breath that signaled a panic attack. His heart started thumping and his lungs tightened like fists. Don't panic, he told himself, swallowing and sucking in deep breaths and letting his shoulders and arms hang limply the way the therapist at the Rehab Center had taught him whenever his heart and lungs acted up on him like this. Don't panic, he always told himself, relax and drink the air, like sucking a thick milkshake through a straw, easy does it, close your eyes, one breath at a time, stay calm.

Usually an attack lasted no more than half a minute, but today it took longer, probably because of the dust in the air. After a while his heart slowed and he could breathe once again.

But the attack had left him feeling wrung out. Anxiety made the room press in on him once more, and he felt a strong claustrophobic desire to be out in the fresh air. He rolled quickly to the door and jerked it open. Hidden behind a bank of shelves labeled "Classics of English Literature," the archives room was a place of almost guaranteed safety from intrusion. He wheeled out of the archives room, past "Classics" and down the length of the library towards Miss Pringle's desk at the far end, near the exit. By the time he reached the librarian the feelings of anxiety were gone and he was ashamed. He had panicked. Get a grip, Mike Scott, he told himself.

The librarian was a thin woman with sad eyes and wispy gray hair, who always wore a black dress. Twenty minutes ago she had offered to push him into Archives, but he had refused, telling her he could manage just fine. "Are you sure you'll be all right?" she had asked. "Let me open the door for you at least." Again he'd refused, holding out his hand impatiently for the big old-fashioned key. He preferred to do things for himself even though opening doors could be difficult. The librarian had stood by, watching him open the door, wringing her thin hands together helplessly.

But now he did need her help.

"Miss Pringle?" he barked.

She looked up from her desk. "Yes, Mike?"

"I need a vacuum cleaner," he snapped at her. "The dust is killing me in there."

She looked at him with her sad eyes, noticing the dirt on his clothes. "You are a mess," she clucked sympathetically. "I could ask one of the janitors to vacuum the room for you tonight when they come on shift; that's the best I can do. Union rules. Though I really don't like anyone going in when I'm not here. I'll try and get Joe; he's reliable."

"He mustn't disturb the books and papers."

"He'll be careful."

"And it's dark in there. I can hardly see what I'm doing. I need a desk lamp."

"I'll make sure a lamp is put in there for you."

Without thanking her, he swiveled away, back to the archives room. He felt fine now. He must try harder to resist those panic attacks, he told himself. He wheeled over to the file box he'd left on the table, and opened it up. Photographs, hundreds of them it looked like, were squashed together inside. He closed the cover and examined the outside of the box for a contents label. There was none. He opened the file again and spread a handful of photographs out on the table in front of him. Most were candids, original snapshots. He pushed them back in the box; it might be easier to examine the pictures in the yearbooks; at least they had a date.

Moving slowly, taking it easier this time, thinking about disturbing the least amount of dust as he possibly could, he slid the box back into its original position on the shelf and looked around for a new place to start. The newspapers perhaps. So many years, so much history.

What he needed was a plan of organization. He thought for a few minutes, elbows on the table, chin in hands. He could write the school history in chapters of decades maybe: Carleton High of the fifties, sixties, and so on. Fifty years. Five chapters. The school really *was* old. Ancient. The archives room was like a tomb. Tombs were scary places. He glanced at the door. It was closed. He felt the flesh on the back of his neck prickling.

There was someone behind him. He spun his wheelchair around quickly.

14 . . . because i'm in a wheelchair don't mean i've got to be nice

"Careful!"

A girl slipped back out of his way and then stood, regarding him gravely.

The dark shadows and shades of gray in the room slipped and shifted. Light drizzled through the cobwebbed window and rode the drifting dust motes.

His heart was pounding. He was gripping his wheel rubbers hard; he willed his arms to drop and relax.

The damned kid had scared him.

"Hasn't anyone ever told you not to sneak up on people?" he yelled angrily.

The girl flinched at the force of his anger.

His heartbeat steadied.

Damned kid!

The anger went out of him. He felt weak, drained. He said quietly, "I didn't hear you come in."

She said, "What happened to your legs?"

"Did you hear what I said?"

Instead of answering she came closer to the wheelchair, examining him boldly. "What happened to your legs?" she asked again.

Wasn't the answer obvious? Stupid kid! "I don't *have* any damn legs."

"Why not? And you mustn't swear."

"Accident. And damn isn't a swear word."

"It is so."

"No, it isn't."

"My name is Sarah. And I know who you are: you're Mike Scott. You're in twelfth grade, a senior. You graduate this year." Her eyes went around the room.

He understood: she was one of the eager beavers from the yearbook committee, sent by Margaret Cowley. Small and skinny, gray eyes, brown hair; that summed her up. Like all the eighth graders, she wore new clothes, bought especially to mark their first year of high school — jeans, shirt, sweater, white socks, runners, and a tote bag. He growled at her. "I told Cowley I don't need anyone."

She made no move to go.

She was holding up the work. "Look, kid … "

"Sarah."

" … I've got work to do … "

"I've come to help you."

"I told you. I don't need anyone."

"Everyone needs someone. Parents, for instance; everyone needs parents."

"I've got no parents."

"Everyone's got parents." She thought for a second. "Unless you're an orphan."

"I've got work to do. So get lost."

"You're not very nice."

He scowled. "Just because I'm in a wheelchair don't mean I've got to be nice."

She stood watching him, saying nothing.

He growled, "Don't you have a class to go to?"

"Michael is a nice name even if you're not so nice."

"It's not Michael, it's Mike."

"I like Michael better. It's more … dignified."

He scrunched up his face into his most powerful, sure-fire scowl. This one always worked; people left him alone. But not this kid.

"What is the *stuff* you've got to do?" she asked.

"Write a history of the school." To his own ears he sounded self-important, like Margaret Cowley, and felt disgusted with himself.

"I've come to help you," she said again, moving forward and stroking a wheel rim of his chair. Her fingers were long and white, like chalk.

"There must be something wrong with your ears, kid. You want me to spell it out for you? *I don't need help*. So get lost."

She stepped back. "My name is not kid, it's Sarah."

"I've got work to do, so be a good girl and go play on the railway track."

Her gray eyes darkened. "But I *want* to help you."

She seemed upset, watching him, saying nothing for a while, and then she said, "It must be tough, sitting in a wheelchair all the time."

"You get used to it."

She probed for details. Would he always be in a wheelchair? Couldn't he get artificial legs? Was it hard to get out of the chair when it was time to go to bed? How did he manage to go to the bathroom? What was it like looking up at people all the time?

Instead of answering he waited until she had run out of breath and then he growled, "You finished?"

She was immediately contrite. "Sorry, Michael, really I am. I get carried away sometimes. My mother says — "

"Okay already! If you stop with the questions and keep your mouth shut I'll let you help."

"Gee, thanks. I won't say anoth — "

He interrupted her, pointing. "Do you think you could reach those books off the top shelf?"

"Of course." She climbed up on the stool, took down the books and dropped them gently onto the table below.

He growled, "You can come for a few minutes tomorrow if you like. Get stuff down off the shelves for me."

His acknowledgment of her usefulness seemed to please her. She became more animated, sitting on the edge of the table and swinging her jeans-clad legs. "Helping will be fun."

"I've got to go through all those old newspapers." He pointed to the high shelves. "And I need to find one of each yearbook starting from 1950 when Carleton first opened its doors."

"I can do that for you." She started rooting around among the yearbooks, her clothes already begrimed with dirt, no longer new and spotless. He remembered how Becky, starting the day off with clean clothes and shining face, was often a disaster area by noon.

They worked together. Mike toiled through his bundle of newspapers; Sarah gathered yearbooks, stacking them in order of date on one of the lower shelves. The bell went for second period. He could hear it far away throughout the school, on the other side of the closed door. "Come on, kid. Gotta go."

She skipped ahead and held the door open for him as he wheeled through. He turned, locked the door and hung the key on its hook in the librarian's office. Sarah grabbed the handles of his chair and moved him towards the library door.

"I don't like being pushed," he yelled angrily over the noise coming from the hallway outside.

But she ignored his objection, pushing even harder.

Being pushed by an eighth grade girl was a major embarrassment. He felt himself propelled out the library door and into the crowded corridor. The chair stopped.

Mike swiveled around to tell her never to do that again, but he was too late, she'd gone. He craned his neck, searching back along the hallway, but she had disappeared into the crowd.

15 . . . vanished from the face of the earth

The next day was Friday.

The archives room had been vacuumed; much of the dust and dirt was gone, though he was sure there would be more once he started moving the newspapers about. But for now breathing was easier. And Miss Pringle had supplied a desk lamp.

Sarah didn't come. Too bad. He knew he hadn't been too nice to her yesterday and felt a twinge of guilt.

He started work. Maybe she would come tomorrow. No, tomorrow was Saturday. Oh, well, maybe Monday.

His aunt had let him have her portable radio, an old-fashioned thing in a worn leather case — a Walkman would be better, but a Walkman was expensive. He set his aunt's radio down on the desk, plugged in, switched on.

" ... *Egyptian airliner crashed into the sea shortly after taking off from Kennedy airport, killing all 217 people on board* ... "

Instant death.

The radio was set to his aunt's gloom-and-doom station.

He twisted the dial to a music station and started work, trying not to think of 217 people in an airliner vanished from the face of the earth, all dying in the same instant.

On Monday Sarah didn't come again. Margaret Cowley had probably assigned her to a different job; or her classroom teacher had put her foot down, insisting she attend class; or she didn't like the archives and had refused a second day working in the dust; or she simply didn't like him. No problem; he didn't need a girl anyway. He would ask Miss Pringle for help if he needed materials off the upper shelves.

He worked and listened to his radio.

Later that evening as they were slurping their milkshakes in the Dairy Queen, Robbie wanted to know what the eighth grader was like.

"She was just a kid," said Mike. "Nothing special. She came once and hasn't been back."

"You probably scared the spaghetti out of her."

"What are you saying, Robbie? Cripples are scary?"

Robbie recoiled from his friend's sudden anger. "Take it easy, Mike. I wasn't saying anything of the sort. You know me better than that."

"Sorry, Robbie. I don't know what's the matter with me."

"What's her name?"

"Look — the kid only came the once. I told you: she quit already."

"But you remember her name, right?"

"I told you. Sarah."

"Sarah what?"

"She didn't say. People do that, just tell their first names. Anyway, it doesn't matter. She didn't like the job, I guess. No big deal. You know how girls are: they hate to get dirty."

"Was she big, small, medium, good-looking, ugly, what?"

Mike said, "I didn't really notice. Small, I think. All the eights are midgets."

"No way," said Robbie. "These days? Eighth graders come in all sizes."

They finished their shakes and Robbie ordered his usual bag of fries chaser.

He was surprised when Sarah showed up on Tuesday. She was more subdued, less talkative, seeming to sense his desire for silence and solitude. He felt more depressed than usual; he didn't know why. Life was a drag. You had only to look around. Innocent people were killed by stupid, irresponsible, not-fit-to-live drunks; many people had nothing, while others had everything; or they died young, in wars or in airplanes falling from the sky, like that Egyptian plane the other day; or they died from starvation or terrible diseases, while others lived to be eighty or ninety or a hundred without ever being sick or missing a meal their entire lives. Life was senseless and unfair: life was the pits.

Sarah worked quietly, not bothering him, tidying the *Clarion*s, returning loose copies to their proper bundles, retying and restacking, moving about soundlessly as though in a sick room.

She didn't even say goodbye; just before the bell he looked over at the other side of the dimly lit room and she wasn't there, had escaped a few minutes early, no doubt, to gossip with her locker partner or do herself up in the washroom mirror.

She was several minutes late on Wednesday. Girls spent a lot of time in washrooms, he knew that, or they chattered and giggled together at their lockers long after the bell had gone. "Thought you'd decided to take a day off," he grumbled.

She smiled, but said nothing and sat in her usual place at the table with her denim tote bag and took out a sketch pad and pencil box. "Do you need anything from the shelves, Michael?"

He shook his head and turned the radio up.

After a while she said, "Michael, could we have the radio off so we can talk a little while we work?"

"There's nothing to talk about. Besides, I need to concentrate."

"There's plenty to talk about; for instance ..."

He turned the radio up some more.

She reached over, grabbed it, turned it off and put it beside her on the floor, smiling at him cheekily across the table. She had nice teeth, small and white and even.

He narrowed his eyes at her threateningly. He hadn't really wanted the music so loud anyway, and if truth be told didn't mind the silence, but he wasn't about to let her know that. "Look, kid! You better put — "

"Michael, be nice. Here, have some of my Snickers bar." She broke her chocolate bar in half and proffered the package.

He took it. Chocolate was hard to resist.

She began to sketch.

"You're supposed to be helping me."

"I *am* helping you, Michael."

"No. you're not. You're just having yourself a good time."

"What would you like me to do?"

"Well, you could help by looking through these newspapers and searching for interesting stories."

"I'd love to search for interesting stories."

"Slap a Post-It on anything you find. No reports on school dances — unless something unusual happens, like a fire or a fight, or problems with liquor; and no sports or athletics, unless school or district records are broken, or something unusual happens, okay?"

They settled down to work. After a while, Sarah started to hum. He waited for her to stop, but she kept it up. "You're humming," he told her.

"No, I'm not."

"You *were*." He knew how sneaky girls could be with verb tenses. He'd been caught before, with Becky.

"Wasn't."

"You were. You were humming."

"Wasn't."

"Was."

"That should be *were*."

"What were you humming?"

"Beethoven."

"There, you see. You admit it!"

"No, I don't."

He sighed and tried to ignore her.

On Thursday the librarian said, "I've left the door open for you, Mike." Miss Pringle had found a way to help without being pushy. "If you need material from the high shelves I can have one of the library students get it for you."

He didn't thank her as he wheeled past the check-out counter, turned right at Myths & Folklore and headed down to Classics. A left turn, a right and another left brought him to Archives. He pulled the door closed behind him.

"Hello, Michael."

She was already there, sitting at the table with paper, crayons and glue, making colored labels for the newspaper shelves.

16 . . . meant to be together

She looked slightly different, but he couldn't see exactly why. Probably her hair: girls were always fooling around and doing different things with their hair.

She stopped what she was doing and moved to the stool, where she perched, chin cupped between her hands, big happy smile, elbows on knees, feet on the rung of the stool, saying nothing. She was evidently waiting for him to acknowledge her, to greet her, to say something nice about her colored labels perhaps.

But he only mumbled in his gruff voice, scowling, not wanting to give her the satisfaction of noticing she was on time.

She held something up for him to see. "Look, I brought my paint box."

He wheeled past her to the table. "You can put these newspapers back on the shelf. I've finished with them."

"Don't be such an old grouch, Michael. It's no use pretending you're not glad to see me because I know you are." She slid off the stool.

He watched her: thin, straight back, tumble of abundant dark hair to her shoulders. It was a different style, he was almost certain of it; girls did tricky things with wigs and hairpieces these days, made themselves appear to have more hair than they actually had. She was gluing her new labels to the shelves. They looked good. Nobody would have any trouble in the future looking for specific years.

And the room seemed different today, warmer and brighter, pushing the shadows back, burnishing the mahogany of the table, bathing the bundles of old newsprint in a bronze glow.

"How do you like it?" She stood back, admiring her work.

"It's fine."

She smiled. "Is that all you can say? 'It's fine'?" — mocking his grumpy tone — "I pour my artistic talents into making this place bright and cheerful and organized and all you can — "

"All right! It's great. How's that?"

"'Great' is better. Thank you."

Remembering Robbie, he said, "What's your last name anyway?"

She stepped down off the chair. "Francis. Sarah Francis. My mother's name before she married my father was Frances Finkleheimer, but now it's Frances Francis. Don't you think that's neat?" Without waiting for an answer she said, "I brought my paint box so I can paint you. I'm quite a good painter. You can sit for me."

"I don't want to 'sit' for you."

She pulled a face. "What a sourpuss. I hope I'm

not like you when I get to be a senior." She sighed. "Let's not work today, Michael, okay? Look, I know a good game. I love movies — don't you just love movies? — except I don't get to go too often because of piano practice every day, early in the morning and then again later, in the afternoon, but I don't mind, not really, I love the piano. The game is you pretend to be someone famous, like a movie star and I ask you questions and try to guess who you are, okay?"

"Look, kid …"

"Sarah."

"I don't have time for games. There's a deadline. The yearbook committee is breathing down my neck. I've got to have this project finished for soon after Christmas. My history teacher wants a Carleton fiftieth anniversary research essay handed in as an assignment for his stupid course, get the picture?"

"Could we talk, then, just for a little while, and then you can work?"

Kids were a pain, especially girl kids; all they ever *did* was talk. His scowl didn't even slow her down.

"I want to ask you about fate. Do you believe in fate, Michael? Like two people meant to be together? Like Paris and Helen of Troy? Or Romeo and Juliet? I do." She opened her eyes wide and stared into his. She put on a deep, husky voice, probably copying some screen actress. "You're very good-looking, you know."

He blushed. "Cut it out!"

She laughed. "But you are, Michael. You look like Harrison Ford. So stern and serious and cute. Did you see him in *Raiders of the Lost Ark*? He was so cool. I just loved him."

Before he could tell her to shut up so he could work, she said, "I saw it twice, the first time with my mom and dad and the second time with Jennifer Galt, my best friend." She was silent for a moment, thinking. Then she said, "Michael, if I grow up as fast as I can, will you promise to wait for me?"

"Huh?"

"So we can graduate together."

"Oh, sure. I'll wait for you," he growled sarcastically, looking down at his legs. "I won't be going anyplace."

She touched the places below his knees, the stumps. "Can you feel it when I touch you there?" She was serious now.

"Yes, of course I can."

"Do you miss the feelings you used to get in your legs?"

"Sometimes it feels like they're still there, and I look, expecting to see them. I get shin pains. And sometimes I can wiggle my toes."

"But that's impossible!"

"It's called phantom limbs. Sometimes my brain thinks they're still there."

"Do you feel phantom limbs now?"

"No, only sometimes."

She trailed away from him to sit on the edge of the table, legs dangling, head tilted, face pale and suddenly melancholy. She opened her paint box, picked out a brush and ran a fingertip and thumb over its bristles. "How did it happen? The accident. Was that when you lost your parents and became an orphan?"

The sun inserted a beam through the narrow window. Blue dust motes swam in the air above Sarah's head as he thought back to last year when they had been driving home from the Abbotsford Air Show. They were all tired. Becky was overtired — overexcited, his father had said. His mom called Becky a tomboy because she was sometimes wild, and she loved airplanes as much as Mike. Becky always argued with her mother, saying, "Calling someone a tomboy is so stupid, I'm just a girl." For both Mike and Becky the highlight of the air show had been sitting in the cockpit of a Spitfire. For their father, an ex-navy pilot, it had been the helicopters.

"We were on our way home in the car," he said simply. "A drunk driver hit us head on."

Why was he telling this to a kid? Because sometimes Sarah didn't seem like a kid, that was why; sometimes she seemed quite grown up.

"It was just over a year ago. My parents and my kid sister were ... they were wiped out ... killed. I was sitting in the back seat with my sister. I had my seat belt on. She didn't. But I was trapped, couldn't move. I don't remember much of it. It took a long time, but they got me out; my legs were crushed, below the knees." He shrugged. "That's it."

That was it: a short, simple story. What he didn't tell her was how the simple story, the part he did remember, the part he'd never forget, played and replayed itself in his head most nights before he went to sleep. In detail. With sound effects. Saturday afternoon, middle of August, Dad driving west, sun visor down against the late afternoon brightness, car radio playing some of Mom's favorite music, live every Saturday from New York, that week an opera called *Aïda* — he even remembered the title — Mom with her head back, eyes closed, Becky — still high from an exciting day — giggling, unruly as usual, mimicking the soprano, showing off for Mike's benefit. "Becky!" Mom's testy voice the last thing he heard before the blackness.

Robbie missed being killed. He had arranged to go with them, but canceled out at the last minute, calling early on Saturday morning to say his mother wasn't well; Mrs. Palladin had been up most of the night with pains in her head and stomach, and he was going to stay home and make sure she was okay.

Robbie had never discussed it with Mike, had never acknowledged his lucky escape.

Fate: some live, some die. Yes, he believed in fate all right.

Sarah said, "So who takes care of you? Your grandparents?"

He shook his head. "There aren't any. I live with Aunt Norma, my mother's sister."

"Why?"

"She wanted me. And she's the only relative I have."

"What is your sister's name?"

"Becky."

"How old was she?"

"Ten."

The sunbeam had lasted only a few seconds and now, for some reason — perhaps the thought of Becky dying so young, before her life had really started — the archives room seemed cold and gray. The old newspapers and books and files that before had seemed to him a historian's delight now seemed like so much trash. The whole mess should be thrown out, he thought, and burnt to ashes. In his mind he saw a mountain of paper burning in a huge fire, saw the black-and-white pictures brown and curl as hundreds of smiling crewcut boys and beehive-haired girls blistered into spirals of smoke and flame.

But the room evidently didn't seem cold and gray to Sarah. "What's your favorite food? Mine's chocolate ice-cream." She swung her legs restlessly, a little kid once more.

It was amazing how one minute she could be so grown up and then the next minute be a child again. No, it wasn't amazing, it was annoying. And frustrating. Just when he was talking seriously, she started acting like a stupid little kid, changing the subject, asking childish questions. He was sorry now he'd told her about the car crash; he had never really talked about it to anyone, not even to Robbie or Norma.

"I don't have a favorite damn food."

"Everybody has a favorite food, Michael. Don't be so grouchy. And you must stop swearing like that."

"I'm not grouchy."

"Yes, you are."

"No, I'm not!"

"Then prove it. Tell me your favorite?"

"I refuse to discuss food." Now he sounded like a jerk.

She got up and started leafing through the yearbooks on the shelves, turning her back to him.

"And you're stopping me working."

She made no reply, carrying on as though she hadn't heard him.

He felt a stab of annoyance. He was wasting time. The school history would never get done at this rate. He started reading through a pile of newspapers, but couldn't concentrate with Sarah moving about the room, even though she was silent. Kids! He grabbed a bundle of newspapers for reshelving off the desk, but moved too quickly and lost his balance. Sarah spun around as he fell out of the chair onto the floor, dropping the bundle. He swore loudly. Sarah rushed over to help him, but he pushed her away, explaining to her how to apply the brakes while he clambered back into his seat. He was angry with himself, allowing a kid to see how awkward and helpless he was.

"Are you all right, Michael?"

"Of course I'm all right. I'm used to falling. It's nothing." He felt like a fool.

The bell rang. Another fast seventy-five minutes gone. He retrieved his notebook and slid it into his pack. He hadn't got a lot done this morning; maybe he should tell her not to come so often. He wouldn't have fallen if he hadn't been so annoyed with her.

She stood, watching him. "G'bye, Michael."

Before he could say anything she had hurried out of the room ahead of him. When he got to the hallway she had disappeared into the milling crowd of students.

17 . . . a secret

"Robbie, do you think I look like Harrison Ford?"

Robbie laughed. "Harrison Ford is an old guy. Been around a long time. *Dead Heat on a Merry-Go-Round* was his first movie, in 1966. That's like, what? Thirty-four years ago? Ford played a hotel bellboy, a bit part. The guy must be way over fifty by now."

"You're not answering my question."

"Do you look like Harrison Ford? Hardly. More like Donald Duck, I'd say."

Mike ignored the humor. They were on their way home along the False Creek sea wall. The city was hidden in a thick broth. Foghorns wailed. Robbie pushed Mike's chair off the cement and onto the grass, through sodden leaves, seeking the thickest piles, plowing vigorously, puffing with the effort, while Mike squinted into the fog and gathering darkness from under the peak of his baseball cap. Robbie might be a little on the heavy side, but he was strong, with big arms and wide shoulders.

Robbie said, "I like Harrison Ford. Even if he is an old guy he's great. I'll tell you a secret, Mike, but you're not to tell anyone, okay?"

"What do you think — I can't keep my mouth shut?"

"Sorry, man. But whenever I think of my dad — I never told anyone this — I see him as Harrison Ford. Pretty stupid, huh?"

"No, Robbie, I don't think it's stupid."

Robbie had never known his father. His father was a mystery. All Robbie knew was that he was an engineer and had gone to work in Argentina on a special project when Robbie was a baby. He never returned. His letters stopped suddenly. Enquiries led nowhere. He had disappeared. Robbie's mother believed he was dead.

"I kinda see my old man as Indiana Jones — like in *The Temple of Doom*. You know what I mean? Dangerous adventures and fighting hard to get back home but being prevented by the bad guys."

"Yeah?"

"Yeah. But he'll never come back. I know that, really."

"You never can tell."

"Yeah, well. Why don't you come over to my place this weekend? We could watch *The Temple of Doom* together."

"Sure. Good idea."

"Indiana Jones is the greatest. So you think you look like Harrison Ford?"

"No. Sarah Francis said I look like him."

Robbie grinned. "Ha! She came back. You didn't scare her off after all. So now you know the kid's full name, huh?"

Getting no response, Robbie continued chattering on about Harrison Ford. Whenever he discussed movies his face shone with manic delight. His memory was prodigious, photographic almost. Now his face went into shining transfiguration mode. "*Raiders of the Lost Ark* was 1981. That was a good year for movies. Lots of people thought *Raiders* should've got the Academy Award for Best Pic, or even *Reds* or *The French Lieutenant's Woman*; instead a Brit movie called *Chariots of Fire* got it. Crazy. Ask most kids about *Chariots of Fire* and they won't know what you're talking about — you ever heard of *Chariots of Fire*? — right, nobody has, but mention *Raiders of the Lost Ark* and they'll know right off. I mean, everyone's seen *Raiders*, right? What does that tell you? Also, if you want my opinion, Meryl Streep should've got Best Actress that year, instead of Katherine — "

"Robbie!"

"Sorry. Anyway, Harrison Ford made three Indiana Jones movies: after *Raiders* in '81 there was *Temple of Doom* in '84 and *The Last Crusade* in '89. After that, he — "

"Robbie!"

"Keep you shirt on. Anyway, I'm not telling you any more until you tell me more about your slave girl."

Mike growled, "There's nothing to tell. She helps me, that's all. Pain in the butt most of the time."

"So, where does she live?"

"I didn't ask her. Hey! Would you mind staying on the sea wall and not driving through the hydrangeas? I'm getting showered with bits of twiggy garbage and dead flowers."

"I don't know why I put up with your obnoxity, man. I push you home; I give you the benefit of my razor-sharp memory and mind, and all I get is your personality disorder problems."

"You do it because you're my pal, Robbie. And because you're a good guy."

"I guess."

"Hey, Robbie?"

"What?"

Mike grinned. "Is there really such a word as obnoxity?"

18 . . . death and destruction

He thanked Robbie for the bumpy flight home, dodged through scaffolding and piles of new siding sitting out on Commodore Road and let himself in to his co-op building. The reconstruction work — fixing the leaks — was, incredibly, still going on after eight or nine months. The contractors worked for only a couple of days at a time and then, like migratory birds, disappeared for long periods of time. Then they returned for a day or two or three and disappeared again. The huge blue tarps had become a familiar part of the building.

He fought his way over the cables and construction detritus, took the elevator up to the third floor, unlocked the apartment door and wheeled into his room. Norma wouldn't be home until late. She worked long hours for the Vancouver School District as a Human Resources Supervisor. Sometimes she didn't get home until seven or eight, and often worked Saturdays.

" ... *more than seven thousand dead ... Indian coastal state of Orissa ... fiercest cyclone in twenty-*

*eight years ... worker at the Xerox company in Honolulu
shot and killed seven of his colleagues ... "*

The radio, left on as usual. Norma believed
thieves would hear the radio and think that someone
was home. It was the first thing that greeted him when
he got through the door.

" *... dug up more than two thousand bodies . . . Kosovo
... mass graves."*

Death and destruction.

Chaos and turmoil.

A normal day. He reached up to the kitchen shelf
to switch off the radio, but the shelf was too high and
he overbalanced and fell to the floor, cursing. By the
time he was back in his chair and had switched off
the radio he was sweating from the effort.

His room was small. All the co-op rooms were
small, and many had leaks or damp patches, including Norma's room, which had a swath of ugly gray-
green stains on its outside wall and ceiling. But Mike's
room was okay; there were no damp patches and he
appreciated the handicap aids, like his room's automatic pocket door and the special frame over his
bed and the extra handrails in the bathroom.

The building's tenants were okay too, not that
he ever spoke to any of them much except he usually
said hello to the Dhaliwals across the hall — Dolly
and her husband, a big man with a beard and tur-
ban, and their two small children whose names he
didn't know — and a man in a wheelchair on the
main floor whose name was Chris Telford. Mike
usually just kept his head down, and if anyone tried
to start a conversation he did his scowl-and-growl

routine; that usually shut them up. If this failed he simply turned his back on them, swiveling his chair rapidly away; that always worked.

Chris Telford drove an old Lincoln with special hand controls because his legs were paralyzed. Chris still had his legs, even though they were no good to him. Dead-weight, like a ball and chain, thought Mike, who considered himself better off than Chris because without the weight of his lower legs he could swing himself about and lift himself up more easily. Even though there was a twenty-year difference in their ages Mike and Chris were friends. Chris had already given Mike several driving lessons, but progress was slow: it would take hundreds of repetitions, Chris said, before the hand controls would become instinctive. Not that there was ever any immediate hope of Mike owning his own car. But some day maybe ...

He gripped the steel bars over his bed, pulled himself up out of his chair, and swung on to his bed. His arms and shoulders were getting stronger. It was always good to lie down, for his behind was always sore by the end of the day from the constant sitting. Some of that soreness often developed into blisters, like bedsores, and he had to be careful they didn't become infected.

Norma had gathered up most of the junk from his old room and put it aside instead of storing it with everything else, so that Mike's co-op room was decorated with his old airplane posters. Hardly any actual wall or ceiling showed; there was everything from CF-18 to B-29, Messerschmitt to Mustang,

Stealth to Spitfire, Hurricane to Wellington, F16 to Hawker Harrier. There were even ultralight posters he'd obtained from the manufacturers: a Weedhopper, an Avenger and an Aero-Lite 103.

The rest of the room, though, was untidy: a torn and damaged map of Tolkien's Middle-earth hung askew under a Sopwith Camel biplane poster; CDs and cassettes, escaped fugitives from plastic cases, lay scattered about the floor; a collection of *Clarion*s and a couple of yearbooks from the archives decorated the furniture — the chest, a chair, and bookshelves, which were also messy with sci-fi and fantasy paperbacks in heaps and framed snapshots of Mom and Dad and Becky. At least there were no dirty socks, he thought, and no shoes; he wouldn't be needing footwear anytime soon. "Some people are just naturally disorganized," he had once explained to Robbie, who always kept his stuff neat.

He was tired. He closed his eyes and, as usual, thoughts of his lost family came to mind. Becky laughing and happy, just the way she was seconds before the crash. The sounds came back to him: soprano on the car radio; Becky giggling and singing. His mother's voice, "Becky!" Blackout.

He missed them and he missed his strong legs and it was like he was hollowed out and empty because so much of his life had been stolen from him.

Thoughts of his father: William J. Scott. Will Scott. Husband of Joanne Scott. Proud father of Michael and Rebecca. Dad. When he was little he had sometimes visited his dad's real estate office, Saturday mornings, helping, churning out information sheets on the copy machine while his dad made preparations for open houses and appointments. Mike liked it there. His dad's co-workers came and went, telephoned, faxed, e-mailed, talked to Mike, joked with his dad, complimented Mike on the good work he was doing, reminded his dad how lucky he was to have a son old enough to help. Mike enjoyed the praise, smiling up at his dad, waiting for him to praise him too — just a word would do — but it never came. When Mike was older, his dad watched him run at track meets. Mike would look out for him in the crowd and wave shyly when he saw him standing there. His dad always waved back, but carelessly, it seemed to Mike, without the same enthusiasm he thought he saw from other dads. His mom and Becky came sometimes, especially if it was an important meet, and they would yell and cheer him on. Becky was a neat kid; they all spoiled her, especially Dad. She could do an ear-piercing whistle as good as any boy and did cartwheels and cheerleader routines on the sidelines while yelling his name. She looked a lot like her mother: fair hair, freckles, wicked grin.

Becky. Always a handful, their mother often said with a sigh, even when she was a little kid of four or five, when their mother used to take them in the summer to Granville Island Market to shop and eat ice cream and sit to listen to the musicians in the square. Becky, never still, was always spilling ice cream on her T-shirt or falling and scraping her knees. He remembered the way she used to sail into his room without knocking, throwing herself onto his bed, bugging him with questions, criticizing his taste in clothes, indulging in long monologues about her life and her problems — freckles were a major concern. He never thought he would, but he missed all that.

Now they were gone. He would never see them ever again. He wished he was with them, wherever they were.

The Lysander airplane poster blurred and swam in front of his eyes. He felt sleepy. Usually, if he rested after school, which was most days, it was never for more than twenty minutes, enough time to rest his aching body and recharge his batteries for the evening ahead. Norma would soon be warbling her usual, "I'm ho-o-o-me!" as she came through the door.

When his family had lived up on the Fairview Slopes, not far from the Leinster Co-op, Mike had known very little about his aunt. In those days she was simply a pleasant woman who had never married, who shopped and had lunch with his mother downtown a couple of times a month, who joined the family for dinner at Christmas and Thanksgiving, who had seemed to Mike quiet and undemonstrative. Now he knew Norma as a person who helped people — some of the seniors in the building, for example, picking up their prescriptions from the pharmacy, or food from the Safeway, or helping fill out their income tax forms. People came to her with their problems. As chairwoman of the co-op council, she had also put many hours into the problems of building repair and reconstruction.

He rolled over on his side and reached for his Battle of Britain book on his bedside table. It was a big book with plenty of pictures and descriptions of British, German, American and Japanese aircraft. He turned to the first page and read, for the umpteenth time, Canadian John Gillespie Magee's "High Flight," the sonnet about the pilot slipping "the surly bonds of earth" in his airplane. Slipping the surly bonds of earth could also mean death, Mike now knew, though he hadn't figured it out before.

He read some of the aircraft technical specs for a while, but soon didn't know what he was reading. He couldn't concentrate. The words began to make no sense. He stared up at the ceiling, at the Spitfire escaping the surly bonds of earth and soaring above the clouds into blinding sunlight. He thought of his mom with birds fluttering about her head, then ...

He fell asleep.

16 ... funny kid

He found himself thinking of Sarah occasionally. Funny kid, he thought. Most girls would hate working in the musty, dusty archives, but she seemed eager to help him. It wasn't as if he was doing anything really interesting — reading old books and newspapers and examining old photographs and making notes on a yellow pad — most thirteen-year-olds would have been screaming to be let out of the cage a long time ago.

The first Saturday in December was fine. Robbie dropped over for brunch. Norma made pancakes with butter and blueberry syrup while the kitchen radio, now on a lower shelf where Mike could reach it, traded in tragedies: " ... *hundreds drowned in Vietnam ... death toll for the latest earthquake in Turkey risen to over five hundred ... serial killer in Pakistan claims he killed a hundred children ... *"

Disasters of the Day. Norma's bad stuff; her ears and brain soaked it all up so she could discuss it with her friends in the co-op. GDG — Global Disaster Gossip, Mike called it. Calamities and catastrophes;

tragedy every hour of the day, every day of the week.

Sunday was dry with a smear of sun. Norma packed a picnic for three and, with Mike and Robbie in her Volkswagon, drove out to the Fraser Valley to watch the ultralight flyers taking off and landing. Robbie, though not so crazy about flying, usually went along. He called the flimsy looking aircraft "lawn chairs with wings."

Though he had never been up in an airplane, Mike wanted to be a pilot more than anything. Meanwhile, he enjoyed watching the takeoffs and landings of the ultralights and talking to some of the flyers, a few of whom had become his friends. Some day he would fly; he knew it.

20 ... a glowing red heart

Monday morning. She was late.

"Hi, Michael."

He had just lifted down a batch of *Clarion*s from one of the lower shelves. His strength was steadily improving. "You're late. I've already got half a day's work done," he growled.

"What a liar! Show me what you've done."

He looked at her. Something different? It was her hair again, but this time piled up on her head, making her look older. There was also a new smell. Phew! The stuff these kids sprayed on themselves! Pretty putrid.

"I don't know what kind of perfume you're using," he grumbled, "but you smell like a bubble gum factory."

"Yuck!" She shivered in mock horror. "And I don't know what kind of deodorant you're using, but you smell like ..." She thought hard, rolling her eyes to the ceiling for inspiration. "Pepperoni pizza!" She laughed, delighted with her clever invention. "Come on, Michael, show me this half-day's work you claim to have done already."

He gave up; she hardly ever got mad, no matter how much he insulted her. He pointed. "This school history is starting to get to me; it's so repetitious. Every year there was a big drama or musical production, like *Our Town* or *Oklahoma*. There were dances called sock hops in the fifties, and field trips up Howe Sound or the Fraser Valley. There were special events days, like kids coming to school in their pajamas or in Halloween costumes. Fifty years ago kids used to dress up as Ed Norton or Sadie Hawkins — I had to ask Robbie who these guys were. Then there are sports. Carleton must have had a team for every known sport in existence. They even had a cricket squad when some exchange teacher showed up one year. I know I took on this project initially to get away from my history class, but I also hoped I would find something here in the archives of importance. I mean, what was life like for the average kid? Do these newspapers and yearbooks tell us anything about what it was like to come to Carleton High in those days? I'm not so sure they do. Looking through this stuff I get the impression that each year is the same: the same sports, same dances, same kids. Only the slang words — I plan to supply a list — and the hairstyles are different. I want to include the important changes in the school, if there were any, and in the neighborhood — Fairview Slopes, False Creek. Know what I mean?" He had to stop for breath.

She nodded.

"It makes my job ... it makes writing a history of

Carleton High more of a challenge." He showed her pictures of False Creek taken in the forties and fifties. "I got these from the downtown library. Take a look. Floating shacks on the south shore. Most of them leaked like today's condos. Squatters lived in them all year round."

"What are squatters?"

"Homeless people. Some of their kids came to this school. One of them was a boy named Charlie Johnson. His school record for the high jump still stands; his name is still on the athletics honor roll, and he was also on the academic honor roll. Look, here's his picture."

Sarah examined the picture of a thin, smiling boy with cropped hair, wearing a white undershirt and dark shorts that covered his knees. "Will you put him in your history?"

"You bet I will."

"What about the squatters?"

"I'll put them in too. Charlie was a squatter. They're an important part of the history of the Creek and of Carleton High. Also, I might put in about a candidate for mayor in the 1950 civic election who called False Creek 'a filthy ditch in the center of the city.' He promised to clean it up and run a highway through it."

"What happened?"

"No highway. A guy named Hume got elected and cleaned it up instead. He poured landfill into the space between the shore and Granville Island so it wasn't an island any more — the way it is today. The shacks were all cleared away by 1959."

Sarah crinkled her nose. "I like the bit about Charlie Johnson and the squatters, but the election stuff is boring."

She went around to the other side of the desk and sat on the chair and began painting with her water colors as they talked.

After a while, after they had finished talking about the squatters, he joked, "Sometimes you seem quite sensible, Sarah, not like a girl at all really."

"That is a typical boy remark. Not funny. Anyway, everyone knows girls are more mature than boys."

"No, they're not. That's a popular myth put out by girls."

"Girls are more mature."

"Not."

"Are."

"Then how do you explain the fact that they spend so much time looking at themselves in mirrors, reading magazine articles on how to lose weight and how to look like a film star, and shopping for clothes and jewelry in the mall every weekend, instead of playing soccer or reading good adventure and sci-fi books and watching interesting stuff like "National Geographic" on TV?"

"Girls play soccer as much and as well as boys. And they read everything and do it more quickly than boys, which is why they have time to shop in the mall and read magazine articles."

"Hmmmph!"

"Hmmmph to you, too!" she said happily.

He remembered Robbie's questions. "Where do you live? Are you close to the school?"

"Look," she said, "I'm painting a picture for you to keep."

He craned his neck, but couldn't see much of the picture, only blobs of color.

"Where do I live? Not far. Ash and Seventh. The address is 2230 Ash. Come by anytime and try my mother's shortbread. It's awful. She gives some to everyone who calls. It's crumbly and dry, but she thinks it's wonderful because that's what everyone tells her. It's a very old house, crumbly and dry and awful too, but we like it really. You can't miss it. It's big and white, with green shutters and a deep front porch. My father converted the upstairs into a separate suite, did all the electrical and plumbing himself. The Feinbergs live there. They're nice. They have two kids, Alice and Joel. Alice is eight and Joel is eleven. Do you need anything off a shelf?"

He shook his head. She was funny the way she burbled on, one thought following another in rapid succession. He had finished flipping through the 1975 yearbook and reached for the 1976 — really, there was so little of any historical interest in them.

He glanced at her occasionally as she painted, intent on her work, a tiny frown between her eyebrows, lips pursed in concentration. He thought of Becky.

She must have read his thoughts. "Does your little sister like painting?" She looked up and saw the stricken look on his face. "I'm sorry, Michael. I didn't mean — "

"That's okay. It's just that you made it sound like she's still ... "

She got up and came around to his side of the table and put her hands on his shoulders. "Do you have a picture of her?"

He took out his wallet and showed her Becky's picture.

"She's cute," said Sarah. She studied the picture for a while and then handed it back and returned to her painting.

They talked. She told him about how hard she had to practice piano every day and how much she loved playing, especially loud and fast passages like the ones in the Mozart C Major Sonata. What about pop music? Did she like rock? Of course she did. She burbled on about a band he'd never heard of. Then, as he flipped through yearbooks, he told her about his driving lessons and about the ultralights and how much he wanted to fly. "Most people build them from kits, though you can buy factory-made ones."

"Do they go fast?"

"Fast enough; 120 miles an hour, or faster, depending on the model."

"I love flying. We flew to New York once, to visit my mother's publisher — they paid her expenses. My parents had always wanted to go to New York. Don't you think it's just amazing, Michael, to be flying miles up in the sky with a couple hundred other people, sitting and eating and drinking and reading and going to the bathroom, while the people on the ground don't even know you're there! Will you take me with you in your little airplane, swooping and soaring high above the world, the two of us together. It will be so-o-o-o great!" She laughed, putting the paintbrush down and she clapped her hands together with excitement. "I've *always* wanted to fly in a small plane. Sitting beside you would be so wonderful …"

He shrugged. Why did girls have to get so mushy? Change the subject. "Tell me more about your parents."

She thought for a few seconds, coming down from her high. "Dad drives a delivery van. One Sunday morning I got up early and wore his uniform to bring them coffee in bed, just to make them laugh, and they did; Dad thinks I should be on the stage." Sarah rolled her eyes. "And to listen to my mother you'd think education was more important than a billion dollars. I told you her name is Frances Francis, right? She teaches piano and writes children's music and she talks so fast sometimes I can't keep up with what she's saying and she laughs a lot; excitable, I think, is the word to describe her. She hopes I'll choose a career in medicine, or law, because music doesn't pay very well — unless you get lucky and become a big-name rock star. 'It helps to have money, Sarah,' she always says. I don't care about money, do you, Michael? Music is so much more exciting. Do you play an instrument?"

He shook his head, confused at her rapid questions and subject changes.

"I love the piano. Music is so … " She hunched her shoulders. "Wonderful. I forget myself, forget everything. Someday I will be a famous concert pianist, I know it, and I'll travel round the world giving concerts. Look, see how long my fingers are."

She held up her hands. "I can span a full octave already and I am only — " She stopped, her eyes anxious. "You won't forget to wait for me, Michael, you promised, remember?"

"Huh?"

The bell rang. "I must go, Michael." She gathered her things and ran from the room, leaving him to put away her paints and clean her brush in the sink, under the corroded faucet. He picked up her still-wet painting. At first he couldn't figure it out, but then he saw that it was himself in a shadowy wheelchair. Mike Scott with a dark scowling head and a glowing red heart where his body should be. No legs below the knees.

She didn't really believe all that wait-for-me rubbish, did she?

21 ... the mystery of time and age

The December days were short, dark and cold. The contractors who were supposed to be fixing the condo leaks had not been seen for the past two weeks. They're probably in the Caribbean, on a beach in Cancún, Norma wisecracked dryly to her friends in the co-op.

The history of Carleton was coming along. Mike had made a routine for himself. He would write two histories, he decided: a short snappy one for the yearbook, hitting only the highlights; and a longer one for his history teacher, one that included the less important events, and, of course, footnotes. His pages of notes grew every day, and he was selecting the best photographs from the crammed boxes of original snapshots, trying to match them up with their yearbooks.

He took newspapers, yearbooks and photographs home with him. He studied the faces of students and teachers from thirty, forty, fifty years ago and wondered about the mystery of time and age. He marveled at how a snapshot captured a brief moment of time and preserved it for the future, marveled at how teenage faces and bodies remained ageless and indestructible. He touched with his fingernail the face of a senior boy, captain of the football team in 1951. If he were still alive now he would be about sixty-five years old, a retired pensioner. Some of the kids in the yearbook were probably dead already. Many of the teachers too. Meanwhile their faces and bodies were frozen in time, like Becky in Mike's mind, ten years old for as long as Mike should live to remember her. Or was she aging in some other dimension, carrying on with her life beyond the surly bonds of earth? Or was that just the stuff of fantasy? Becky was dead, but he had to believe he would see her again. And his mom and dad. He had to believe that.

Sarah came every day. He was surprised to discover himself starting to look forward to their ridiculous arguments, to her bright chatter. There were times when she didn't chatter, when she concentrated on her tidying and organizing or her painting instead, and that was fine too, for she filled the dismal room with warmth.

He said to her one day, "Some people die when they're young, like ten or twelve or fifteen." He looked at her to see if he had her attention. He had. She was staring at him with her mouth open and her eyes questioning. He said, "And some people die when they're old, like over fifty." He waited a few beats.

"So?"

"So, do you remember a while ago, talking about fate?"

"Of course."

"Do you think we're all fated to die? At a certain time, and there's nothing we can do to prevent it?"

"I don't know, Michael. Why worry about it?"

He shrugged. "It just seems unfair, that's all; to die young, I mean. It's like you're cheated."

She thought for a few seconds. "I don't think I really believe in fate."

"Why not?"

"I think the opposite, that nothing is planned; everything's ... accidental."

"Accidental?"

"We make things happen ourselves."

"With our free will."

"That's it, our free will." She grinned. "Except for us."

"Huh?"

Her grin grew wider. "You and me. It was fate that brought us together."

She was a contradiction: practical and mushy, serious and funny, helper and nuisance. He was beginning to regret the coming of the weekend when he wouldn't see her.

Saturday morning was the time for Mike and Robbie's usual junk food fix at Granville Island Market. They got the wheelchair as far as the parking lot of Mike's building and saw Chris Telford heaving himself from his wheelchair into his old Lincoln. "You guys wanna lift anyplace?" he yelled.

"Granville Island?" Robbie yelled back.

"I thought you said you needed the exercise," Mike reminded him.

"I need a chocolate fudge sundae more."

Chris's wheelchair wasn't a folder, but had pop-off wheels instead. He popped off the wheels and pulled the chair into the car. "Get behind the wheel," Chris told Mike. "You're driving."

Mike positioned his chair the way he'd seen Chris do it and vaulted into the driver's seat of the Lincoln. Robbie folded Mike's chair, lifted it into the trunk and climbed into the rear seat.

"Start her up and just take it easy," said Chris, handing over the keys.

Before the accident Mike had known how to drive; he had practiced in the family Chevy with his dad. But now it was different; hand controls weren't easy. He had to keep his wits about him and, most of all, had to forget it when his brain was telling his phantom right foot to hit the brake; it meant retraining his brain to signal the hands instead. He had already had lots of practice in Chris's Lincoln and had now reached the point where he felt confident in his ability to control the big car.

Lamey's Mill Road was easy and Granville Island, usually busy, today looked quiet. "Maybe you better take over here," Mike said to Chris when they got to the Anderson junction.

"Not too many people about," said Chris. "You think you could take her onto the island?"

"Sure, I can do it." He drove slowly, over the train tracks, past the Granville Island Brewery and Kids Market and onto Johnston. Traffic was light. He found a parking slot near Bridge's Hotel and braked to a gentle stop. "Phew!"

"I knew you could do it." Chris slapped him on the shoulder.

"Can I open my eyes now?" said Robbie. He lifted Mike's chair out onto the sidewalk, scattering the pigeons.

They always enjoyed the busy ambience of Granville Island with its restaurants, theatres and hotels, its indoor market, its shops and its old-fashioned cobbled streets. In Broker's Bay and in the marinas there were trawlers, gill-netters, charter boats for salmon fishing, kayaks, sailboats, and power boats; in Burrard Inlet, big cruisers and tiny ferries glided to and fro under the bridges; there were even houseboats moored at the boardwalks. The smell of the sea was mixed with the odors of creosoted timbers and French fries. For Mike and Robbie the island was a colorful, exciting place.

"Come on, Chris," said Mike. "I'll buy you a coffee."

"Some other time, Mike. I gotta go. I'm taking Vivian out shopping." Vivian was his lady friend. "You know what, Mike?"

"What?'

"I know it's none of my business, man, but seriously, it's about time you started thinking of prosthetics. Get walking. Get rid of the chair. Drive with legs instead of hand controls. You hear what I'm saying?"

"I hear what you're saying, Chris, and you're right: it's none of your damn business."

"Have it your own way, Mike, but I had to say it. Couldn't rightly call myself a friend if I didn't."

"You did real good on the driving, Mike," said Robbie later, when they were enjoying their sundaes — with a chaser of fries for Robbie — on the open deck among the pigeons. He pointed skyward to a small float plane buzzing down the inlet. "You'll soon be flying one of those suckers, wait and see."

22 . . . a surprise visit

Mike felt stronger and stronger: his more active life had lent new strength to his arms and shoulders. And he felt happier; he didn't know why.

It was now the last week of school before the Christmas vacation. Sarah came to the archives on Monday and they worked and talked together.

"I hate these short dark days," said Mike. "And it's so cold. Winter is a total pain."

"No, it isn't. I like winter. Vancouver might be cold, but it's healthy. And we get snow. Snow is beautiful. We can ski in the mountains. And we get spring showers, fall mists."

"Florida is better."

"No, it isn't. I would hate to live in Florida. Same every day: two kinds of weather, hot and very hot. Two kinds of terrain, flat and very flat. Blah!"

"But better."

"British Columbia rules."

"No, it doesn't."

"Does."

He let her have the last word. It had taken a

while, but Mike had finally figured out that these little arguments were Sarah's way of getting him to talk
and have fun. She didn't mean half of what she said,
would argue black was white just to get something
going between them. Once the simple topics were
dealt with they often moved on to more challenging
ones, like racial equality, pollution and the question
of why there were so many wars. Sarah had opinions
on everything. Talking was easier these days: the yearbooks and newspapers, because they tended to be
uniform and tedious in content, needed only to be
skimmed, a task hardly requiring their full attention.

On Tuesday, Sarah left early, pleading a headache.
She had no sooner gone than Mike had a surprise
visit from Dorfman.

"How is this little history of yours coming along,
Scott?" His pale, magnified eyes searched the table
and the dusty shelves.

Mike showed him what he done so far: the many
pages of notes, the system of organization, the files
and indexes he had set up for the material to be
typed by the committee, the files of photographs to
be included, each photograph numbered and refer-
enced. He had done a lot; the history of Carleton
High was obviously going to be a thorough one.

Dorfman seemed almost disappointed and soon
left.

Sarah was back on Wednesday, her headache gone,
but she tried to persuade Mike that they both needed
fresh air.

"It's this stuffy old place," she said. "Let's take a

day off. You have worked hard; one day off won't hurt."

"Yes, it would."

"No, it wouldn't." Smiling at their usual formula.

"But I …"

"Just for today, please?" she said, gray eyes pleading.

He could take extra work home to make up for the lost time, he thought.

"Where do you want to go?"

"Down to the sea wall." She became excited. "It's my favorite place. The boats in the marina are so colorful, and I love the sound of their bells on a windy day."

"I wouldn't get back in time for my next class."

"You would if you let me help push you."

Mike locked the archives room and they left the school through the back door near the band room. Sarah wore a red ski jacket over a pink sweater and carried her tote bag. "You don't need to push me going downhill," said Mike. "I can manage fine."

A thin fog hung over the Fairview Slopes, False Creek and the Cambie Bridge.

"Tell me more about those little airplanes, the ultralights, you watch at weekends."

"No. You would find it boring."

"No, I wouldn't."

"Okay. There are different kinds, but they're usually made of aluminum tubing, covered in Dacron sailcloth. The Flightstar Spider is one of the best for the money. You can build it yourself. It weighs 145 kilos and it's got a chromoly steel cage and landing gear, comes with a 447 or a 503 Rotax engine. It can do 120k, and depending on your weight, it can take you almost 300 kilometers on a 45 liter tank of gas. Then there's …"

She was wrinkling her nose.

"You're wrinkling your nose."

"No, I'm not."

"You *were* wrinkling your nose."

"No, I wasn't."

"I told you it was boring."

"No, it's not."

"Do you know 'High Flight,' the John Magee poem?"

"I don't think so."

"It's only fourteen lines. Want to hear it?"

"I'd love to hear it."

He recited the sonnet.

"It's beautiful, Michael."

"I imagine flying upward through the clouds and then bursting out into the sunlight, leaving the clouds behind. I call it sunburst. The poem's like that too, I think: it hurls you up through the dark clouds into the sudden brightness of the sun."

They were soon on the sea wall. In the marina, the boats were lurching phantoms in the gray fog.

"Listen to the chimes," said Sarah.

They sat awhile, listening.

"You want to walk along the sea wall to Charleson Park? It's only a short way."

She said, "No. I want to stay here for a few minutes. Then I'll help you up the hill, back to Carleton."

They sat and peered into the fog and listened to

the boat chimes and then they went back.

On Thursday Sarah retied and put away the bundles of *Clarion*s that Mike had finished with while he took stock of his progress in the archives room, going over his notes. His project was looking good. He would have it finished easily before semester's end, in January. Many *Clarion*s were left unexamined — to inspect them all would be impossible in the time available, even with the ones he had been taking to read at home and the ones he had put aside to read over the Christmas holiday — but he was satisfied with the facts he had gathered, the notes he had made.

The next day would be the last school day before the Christmas holiday and the new year. He wouldn't see Sarah for another two weeks. She hadn't talked about Christmas, not once, which was unusual, especially for a girl; girls loved Christmas, didn't they?

"You looking forward to Christmas, Sarah?"

"Christmas?"

She looked blank, like she had never heard of it. Then she said, "Oh, yes, of course." But she didn't sound enthusiastic.

Which was a bit strange, he thought.

23 . . . someone sobbing

He had brought her a Christmas gift, a set of wind chimes that sounded like boats in the marina. He hoped she would like it. He paused at the entrance to the archives room. Miss Pringle had the door open for him, as usual. He heard the sound of someone sobbing coming from inside the room.

The room seemed empty.

He called, "Sarah?"

The sobbing stopped.

He switched on the light. The room was empty.

"Sarah?" As he looked around the room a peculiar feeling slid about inside his ribcage and pinched his heart. The room seemed unnaturally quiet and still. Something was happening. The dusty air felt suddenly charged with electrical particles and he was reminded of the strange feeling he'd had at Halloween with Robbie and his two young cousins. The light dimmed for a few seconds, brightened again and then went out. Don't panic. Probably just a power surge. Knuckles white on his wheel rims, he looked about him. Dust motes that a few seconds ago had drifted thickly in a beam of light from the high window now hung suspended in the air, and the pale gray colors of the room seemed to shift and slide and darken like a black cloud drifting over the sun.

The sobbing started again, louder now.

Then he saw her, huddled on the floor behind the table. He pushed himself in and put an arm around her shoulders. She reached out to him and, kneeling, clung to him, sobbing.

He could see that her jacket was torn, ripped in the back, and her dress also, and that she wore only one shoe.

"Sarah! What happened?"

She groaned and shook her head violently on his chest, clinging to him, face hidden. He pushed her away so he could see her face and she struggled against him wildly. Her face was streaked with mud and tears. He saw now that her torn clothing was dirty and bloody. She pressed herself fiercely against him.

He said no more, but held her until gradually the sobbing subsided and at last she let him go and crumpled to the floor with a sigh of despair.

"Let me help you, Sarah. Tell me ..."

She shook her head wildly and started to cry again. Then she sprang to her feet and fled out the door, limping and stumbling with only one shoe. He hurried after her. When he got to the hallway it was deserted. He wheeled madly along the empty hallway to the office.

"Help!" he yelled.

The startled secretaries stopped what they were doing and stared at him.

"Something's happened," he cried. "An accident!"

Mr. Holeman's door flew open. "What is it?" the principal demanded.

The vice-principal's door flew open, framing a startled Mr. Warren.

"There's been an accident. Sarah Francis. She ran out towards the parking lot. She's hurt bad. Can't get far. Only one shoe. Quick, you've got to find her!"

Mr. Warren rushed out. Mike followed him as Mr. Holeman was giving orders to the secretaries to telephone counselors and maintenance staff.

When Mike got outside — he had to go the opposite way, out the rear of the building and around to the side — he could see nobody in the parking lot. A couple of off-duty teachers appeared. "What's going on?" one of them yelled at Mike. He told them and they ran off, through the parked cars, searching for Sarah. Mr. Warren appeared, saw Mike and hurried over, panting.

"Tell me what you saw."

Mike told him, as quickly and briefly as he could.

"How was she hurt? Was she hit by a car?"

"I don't know."

"You said her name is Sarah Francis, is that right?"

"An eighth grader?"

"Right."

"Go to your class, Mike, and I will know where to find you if I want you. In the meantime I'll have someone check the girl's telephone number and address. Don't worry; we'll find her. She'll be all right."

He didn't go back to class, but sat in the school office, trembling, waiting for news of Sarah.

24 . . . no sarah francis

The principal's office. Norma had been called in from work. She sat next to her nephew. She looked worried.

"You're sure you have her name right?" the principal asked Mike.

"Of course I'm sure! Sarah Francis. You think I'm making it up?"

The conference had been going on for some minutes. Mr. Holeman was asking the questions from behind his desk; Mr. Warren, sitting slightly behind Mike's wheelchair out of view, had so far said nothing. Holeman was a small man with thin gray hair and an easy, confidential manner. Warren, tall, brown hair cut short, tiny mustache, wore a fierce expression and had a stiff military posture. It was now after 4:30, school was out for the Christmas vacation. Mike had been sitting around the office all morning and afternoon. He'd had no lunch, but he wasn't hungry.

Sarah had not been found.

"Let me make sure I have this right," said Holeman

mildly. "Mr. Dorfman has you working in the archives room in the library each morning, first period."

"We've been through all this."

"Please answer. Just to be sure your aunt understands the problem."

"That's right, every morning, first period. I'm writing a history of the school for the yearbook committee." Mike drooped in his chair; he was sore and tired.

"Yes, I understand that, but what about this girl? She's a new student, you say, in the eighth grade. She comes each morning to help. What is the name of her teacher? Whose class would she normally be in at that time of day?"

"How should I know? You have all that information in the school records."

"But we don't. That's the problem. There is no Sarah Francis enrolled at Carleton."

"But she's a student here! I know it for a fact!"

"You say that her parents are John and Frances Francis. But there is no family named Francis in this area."

"That's impossible. They live on Ash Street."

"Who, besides yourself, Mike, has seen this Sarah Francis?"

"Who? Why, everyone in the school! I told you: she's a student here! Miss Pringle sees her every day in the — "

"We have spoken with Miss Pringle. She has never seen this girl in the library."

Mike struck the arms of his chair in frustration. "This is crazy! She must have seen her. What about her teachers? They — "

Norma took his arm. "Take it easy, Mike."

Mr. Warren spoke for the first time. "All eighth graders take English, Mike, as you know. There are three teachers of eighth grade English: Miss Mercer, Mr. Simmons and Mr. Tinley. They do not have a girl named Sarah Francis in any of their classes."

"You're saying I made this all up. You're saying I'm crazy."

"No," said Holeman. "We're not saying that, not at all. But we know you have been under a lot of pressure since your accident and it's possible that you *think* you saw …"

Norma stood. "I think that's enough for now, gentlemen. I'm taking Mike home. He's tired."

Norma pushed him home. He seldom allowed her to push him. Today he didn't say a word.

25 . . . professional help

The Christmas holiday in the Lower Mainland was celebrated under another blanket of fog. Mike couldn't remember any other year being as bad as this one for fog.

He worried about her.

Norma asked a lot of questions, most of which he couldn't answer. She thought they should seek professional help.

"What do you mean, Norma? I should see a shrink?"

"I'm not sure, Mike. But it wouldn't do any harm to explore the idea."

"You think I'm mad."

"No, I don't think you're mad. But we can't figure this out by ourselves, Mike; we need help."

He shook his head. "Sarah is the one who needs help, not me."

He wheeled to his room, but the sound of Norma's radio through the thin door distracted him: " ... *three teenagers killed in a motor vehicle accident in Surrey ... the UN responsibility for failing to prevent the July 1995 massacre of seven thousand Muslims in Srebrenica ... "*

On and on.

"Could you turn that radio down, Norma!" he yelled through the door.

She turned it off.

He stared unseeingly at the mess of *Clarion*s piled around the room, thinking only of Sarah, desperate to do something, but not knowing what. Then he had an idea: he could check her home, the address she had given him, at Seventh and Ash. What was the number? — 2230, that was it. But it was late; he would go in the morning. It wasn't far; with the new strength in his arms and shoulders he could make it in about fifteen minutes.

But the next morning was foggy and he decided to wait until the afternoon.

By the afternoon the morning fog had lost its brightness to become a damp miasma. Visibility was poor. He could wait no longer; he had to go. Saturday was Norma's day for shopping. He took off, pushing himself up the Fairview Slopes vigorously. He was sweating by the time he got there.

Sarah's block of Ash Street was lined with mature horse-chestnuts — bare branched, but dense and shrouded in fog. He located 2230, but it was a modern condo. He obviously had the wrong number. He checked the whole block; they were all condos. There was no house fitting Sarah's description, no big white house with green shutters and a deep front porch.

What did it mean? Sarah didn't know her own

address? Or she had lied to him? It made no sense.

His return journey down the hill was easier, but he didn't really notice.

Norma wasn't home. He went to his room and closed the door.

His mind was spinning. Maybe he *was* going mad. Nothing made any sense.

He started going through a bundle of 1980s *Clarions*, staring at them, but not seeing anything. All he could see and hear was Sarah kneeling on the floor of the archives room, sobbing her heart out.

Norma gave Mike a book for Christmas. It was about flying, written by a Battle of Britain pilot. He glanced at the cover and put it away in his room. He thanked Norma and told her he would read it after Christmas.

26 . . . do you believe?

Robbie had telephoned on Friday, Christmas Eve, and several times on Christmas Day. "Tell Robbie I don't feel like talking," Mike told Norma.

But on Sunday morning, Boxing Day, with Vancouver still trapped under a damp fog, Mike felt a little better.

"You don't look so good, man," said Robbie as he pushed Mike along the sea wall towards Granville Island. "Like you haven't slept for a month."

"I'm okay."

"I heard about ... you know."

"Yeah. Everyone thinks I'm psycho."

"I don't."

They wheeled along in silence for a while. Then Robbie said, "I've been thinking about it all — the girl, Sarah, who was helping you, and I can see how everything you say might be true, like Patrick Swayze — "

"Huh?"

"Patrick Swayze. He was in a movie called *Ghost*, an old flick from ten years ago, and he died and came back to protect his wife, Demi Moore."

Mike stopped his chair. "So who's the crazy one now! What are you saying? Sarah was a ghost!"

"Well, why not?"

"Sarah wasn't a ghost; she was as real as you and me. Anyway, a movie doesn't prove there are ghosts, Robbie."

"Maybe, but there's this other movie called … "

Mike switched off. It would do no good to tell Robbie about Sarah, torn and bleeding and sobbing; to Robbie it was like a movie, fiction, just another story. Robbie was like his aunt; he didn't believe Sarah was real, believed Mike was hallucinating, thought he was bonkers, thought he should see a shrink.

The trouble with Robbie was he loved telling the plots of old movies, blithely unaware that everyone in the world didn't care about some of those old movies; he was downright boring sometimes, but Mike never complained for fear of hurting his feelings. Robbie finally finished explaining the movie's plot and Mike managed to change the subject.

They sat out on the deck at Granville Island Market, eating ice cream. Robbie hadn't bought any fries yet, but Mike knew he would as soon as the ice cream was gone. English Bay lay beyond, hidden in the fog. Mike said, "All those movies about coming back from death, do you believe them, Robbie?"

"I dunno, Mike. Yes and no, I guess. Sometimes I believe; sometimes I don't. I kid myself that my dad will come back one day, either from South America and the bad guys, or from the spirit world.

But mostly I believe it ain't gonna happen, that I'll never meet him and find out what he's like."

"You're a good friend, Robbie. I don't ever tell you that, do I? I don't know what I'd do without you and that's the truth."

He meant what he'd said. He thought of Sarah's painting. Robbie is the one with the big heart, he thought, not me.

Mike lay on his bed. The workers were back again, on Boxing Day for crying out loud! What was it with these guys? Were there no flights to the Caribbean on Boxing Day? The noise of drills and hammers rang in his head, and he really began to believe he *was* going mad.

27 . . . the new millennium

He couldn't stop thinking about her. The long vacation was an unending torment.

On the last day of December the city celebrated the new millennium. It would soon be the year 2000. There were fireworks and music. Norma stayed home, which was what she usually did on New Year's, she said: it was dangerous to be outside, what with the drunken crowds and the fireworks and the traffic and all the carryings on.

He went out alone before midnight, pushing himself through knots of revelers, across Leg-in-Boot Square and down Bucketwheel. The sea wall here was mainly cobblestones and the going was bumpy, with the ever-present danger of falling. He stopped at a bench near the marina and looked down the inlet towards the lights of the Granville Bridge. There were no people here. It had been raining earlier and the ground was still wet. He watched a tugboat pulling a barge loaded with sand towards the Cambie Bridge; some had to work, millennium or not. On the opposite side of the inlet the bright lights of the city, augmented with hundreds of red and green Christmas lights, were like a child's idea of what heaven might look like at night. Did they have night in heaven? he wondered. Any drawings or paintings he'd ever seen showed heaven in sunlight, with great fleecy clouds and sunbeams and white-robed angels with golden harps.

Fireworks exploded on the Fairview Slopes; rockets rode the night sky.

The first day of January wore another heavy gray cloak of unseasonable fog.

It was Y2K, the year 2000. It was supposed to be a techno version of the Black Death. But the world hadn't almost come to an end as many so-called experts had foretold; computer microchips had somehow managed to slide digits efficiently and obligingly from 1 to 2, from 1999 to 2000. Airplanes failed to fall from the skies; telephones and electrical grids did not break down; civilization failed to crumble. Everything, in fact, seemed perfectly normal. No Doomsday, no meltdown, nothing. It was, Mike thought, a little disappointing.

He stayed home, working half-heartedly on an English essay, due soon after the holiday. The semester had been a hard one; taking three heavies like History, Math and English in the same semester had been tough. Then there was the additional eleventh grade work; what was supposed to have been a "few make-up units" had turned out to be a heavy burden: reading *Macbeth* for English, and extra work in math, chemistry and physics, not to mention

Dorfman's history essays. Teachers saw their own subjects as the most important — miss reading *Macbeth*, for example, and your brain would self-destruct. He had kept telling himself that none of it mattered, but ingrained work habits demanded that he do the best he could. In the evening he watched TV with Norma until the news came on. Norma liked to watch the news. He didn't. TV news was as bad as radio news, a continuous litany of tragedy and death. Who needed it? He took his English essay and a few *Clarion*s to his room. The newspapers were on his lap. The headlines on the front page jumped out at him.

His heart froze.

CARLETON STUDENT MURDER VICTIM

BODY OF MISSING TEENAGER FOUND

The search for thirteen-year-old Sarah Francis, missing since the evening of Friday, December 17, 1982, came to a tragic end the next morning when her body was found in bushes near Charleson Park in False Creek.

The Carleton High eighth grader was reported missing by her parents, John and Frances Francis of 2230 Ash Street after she failed to return home from a school debating practice.

Sarah was the Francis's only child. Her funeral will take place on Thursday, 10 a.m., at St. Augustine's church.

The Vancouver Police Department is asking for help

in their investigation: anyone who saw Sarah on the Friday evening, or who saw anything or anyone suspicious is asked to contact the Vancouver Police immediately (more on p.3).

His hands trembled as he examined the date of the newspaper: January 1983, New Year Edition.

A thirteen-year-old girl named Sarah Francis died seventeen years ago.

Murdered.

His heart bursting, he turned to page three. In the center was a picture of Sarah, *his* Sarah, the same Sarah Francis who had helped him in the archives room.

The picture appeared to be her seventh grade elementary school photograph, with a black border around it. She was smiling.

Then followed:

(cont'd from p.1) All of us at Carleton High, students and faculty, mourn the loss of one of our brightest and best. Eighth grader Sarah Francis's brutal murder has caused a loud scream of anger and grief to be heard throughout the city.

Sarah came to Carleton High in September from Sanderson Elementary. Teachers there characterized her as a bright and popular student. A gifted pianist and musician, she was the winner of several trophies for her outstanding performances in music festivals and competitions throughout the Lower Mainland.

Jennifer Galt, her best friend, told the Clarion *in a tearful interview, "Sarah was the kindest and most genuine person I've ever met," and, "I'm going to miss her every day for the rest of my life."*

The Attorney General is calling on the federal govern-ment to institute the death penalty for child killers.

Sarah, torn and bleeding, sobbing wildly. The im-age seared his mind. It was there forever; it would never go away. She had been murdered on Friday, December 17, 1982. He struggled to recall the date of their last meeting, when she was sobbing in the archives room. He remembered: it was also Friday, December 17, the same day and date exactly — except it was seventeen years later, in 1999!

He did not show the newspaper to Norma or to Robbie, but kept the story to himself, saying noth-ing. Instead, he lay on his bed staring at Sarah's watercolor pinned on the wall — the one of him-self in his chair as a dark head and red heart — and at the clouds of his Westland Lysander ceiling poster, thinking of Sarah, hearing again that wild sobbing, seeing her thin body in its ripped dress falling through clouds, falling and falling.

28 . . . hurrying as fast as i can

Century 21. Tuesday, January 4.

Leinster Co-op seemed to exist in an endless state of semi-completion. The repairs were still unfinished. The contractors had added more blue tarps, this time to the east end of the building, and there seemed to be more scaffolding, more ropes, more ladders and buckets. The building was suffocating under its blue mantle; Mike could swear he could hear it sighing and groaning. Outside, the mist and fog continued, everything dark, damp, dull.

Norma spoke with the doctors at Rehab and tried to persuade Mike to cooperate with them, but he refused to go. "I'm not crazy," he said. She brought a psychiatric nurse to the apartment, but Mike refused to speak to her, locking himself in his room and not coming out until the woman had gone.

Norma had started going out once a week, on a Tuesday evening, to a support group at the Rehab Center.

Mike returned to school after the holiday and was happy to be allowed back in his own dusty library room; Mr. Holeman thought it best that he finish what he had started. This time, however, the door was to be left open and someone, Miss Pringle or another staff member, would look in on him from time to time to make sure he was all right.

Sarah did not come.

He missed her.

Later, as he sat in Mr. Talbot's Math class, only half listening to Talbot's gravelly bleat, the door opened and in she walked. Mike blinked and shook his head, not believing his eyes. It was Sarah! She was scanning the faces, searching for him. The sight of her squeezed his chest, made his heart plunge like he was bungee jumping off the Lions Gate Bridge.

Sarah had come back.

She spotted him and walked deliberately across the room and down the aisle. Nobody saw her, he could tell, for she caused not a ripple in the motionless air; Talbot continued his bleating, and the kids went on with their glassy-eyed listening.

She was invisible to everyone in the room except him. Unless he was hallucinating.

But then he heard her voice. "Michael!" Her eyes shone. She smiled, then glanced over her shoulder at the teacher, now writing on the blackboard. "Come outside."

"What...?"

Talbot said, "Are you all right at the back there, Mike?"

"Gotta go to the washroom," he yelled back.

Talbot blinked and nodded.

He followed Sarah out of the classroom — nobody

looked at her — and along the deserted hallway to his locker and took out his jacket. "It's damp outside. Wear this." He handed her the jacket.

She hung it over her shoulders and followed him out across the foggy school quadrangle, down a misty lane of maples to a row of benches decorated with scatterings of yellow-gold leaves. She brushed away a few leaves and sat on a bench facing him, her outline indistinct and shifting as wisps of fog curled about her.

She wore a plain blue fitted cotton dress that made her look older. There was something else different: it was in the way she sat, quiet and composed and serious. Gone was the naïve, excited, motor-mouth kid, chattering about music and painting and arguing about nothing. Aware that he was staring at her, but unable to stop, he was noticing tiny details, like the soft dark crescents of short hair behind her ears curling forward onto the pale skin of her neck, the attractive shape of her mouth and the way she had of biting her lower lip when she was thinking. Everything about her was perfect ... her dark hair, shining and abundantly soft ...

"You're different, Sarah. Older."

She looked pleased. "You promised to wait for me, Michael, remember? I'm hurrying as fast as I can."

"I don't understand, Sarah. Tell me. What ..." Confused and inarticulate, he wheeled closer. "I worried about you, Sarah. You were so ... I wanted to help ..."

She stopped him with a finger to his lips. "You helped more than you know."

She pushed a curl of dark hair back behind her ear.

The fog drifted closer and surrounded them. Her eyes were the same color as the fog. They were alone.

"The others in Talbot's classroom couldn't see you."

She said nothing.

"Nobody ever saw you, did they; even Miss Pringle in the library, she didn't see you either."

She smiled. "You're the only one, Michael."

"You died in 1982. And I looked for your house on Ash, an old white house with green shutters, remember? It isn't there."

She was silent, looking at him with wide gray eyes.

"Sarah? What does it all mean? Why are you here?"

"I came to help you, remember?"

"Yes, but I don't understand any of it, Sarah. How can you be here, older, when you were ... murd — "

She cut him off. "I don't know. But it doesn't matter. What matters is I'm here. That's all; I'm here and we're together."

"Yes." She was right; that was all that mattered: her joyful smile, his feeling of happiness.

"Do you like how I look?" She sat up straight as if for an inspection, a remnant of the childish, playful Sarah.

"You look ... good, Sarah."

"It won't be long, Michael. I'm hurrying for you." She leaned forward and took his hands in hers. "I've missed you. I came back. I wanted you to know."

"Who ... did it to you, Sarah? Was he ... did the police ... ?"

She withdrew her hands. Her eyes darkened and she shook her head. "I told you. It doesn't matter."

"But you know who."

She made no reply.

"Tell me his name."

She shook her head, agitated.

"Why not? If you know who it is then you *must* tell me."

Sarah looked down at her feet.

The fog slid and shifted, closing thickly about them.

"Tell me, Sarah, and I will see he pays. Or *write* his name! Here! Take this branch and write his name in the dirt."

"No. Let me show you." She stood and wheeled him back to the school, through the hallways, to Dorfman's history class. She stood outside the door. She pushed the chair forward into the classroom. The students raised their heads from their note-taking, watching Mike in his wheelchair. Mr. Dorfman looked up from his lighted projector. "Yes, Scott, what is it?"

Sarah raised an arm and pointed at Dorfman. "There, Michael. He is the one."

Mike stared at Dorfman. When he turned back to Sarah she had gone.

25 . . . wouldn't believe me

He telephoned the police that same afternoon, as soon as he got home, and asked the Homicide Department for information on the Sarah Francis murder of 1982. He was asked to leave his name and number; someone would get back to him.

It was early; Norma wouldn't be home for at least two hours.

An hour later a Detective Inspector Samson called. He could not discuss the case on the telephone, but could Mike come downtown to police headquarters in the morning? Say nine o'clock? Or a detective could be sent to his home.

Chris drove him downtown the next morning and dropped him off at the Public Safety Building. He would wait for him in Starbucks across the street.

Samson was a tall thin man with weary brown eyes and bushy gray hair. His clothes were casual: jeans, golf shirt, cable-knit sweater, tweed jacket. The office, or interview room, was small and bare: table, three chairs, picture of the Queen. The detective had difficulty closing the door because of the space taken by Mike's wheelchair. He perched on the edge of the desk and read aloud from a file, his voice a bass rumble. "The body of Sarah Francis, white female, thirteen, was found in Charleson Park, False Creek, December 1982." He looked down at Mike. "Is this the Sarah Francis you were asking about?"

Mike nodded.

"Well?" said Samson. "What can you tell me about this case?"

"I know you didn't catch her killer."

"How do you know that?"

"Because he's still out there."

Samson said nothing, waiting for him to go on.

"I know who killed her."

"Who?"

"My history teacher, Mr. Dorfman."

"You don't say."

"I do say," said Mike calmly.

Samson slid off the desk, opened a drawer and pulled out a tape recorder. "Any objection if we get this on tape?"

Mike shrugged.

Samson spoke into the microphone, recording the date, time and place, and Mike's name, age and address. Then he sat behind the desk. "You're a senior at Carleton High. You say your history teacher, Mr. Dorfman, murdered Sarah Francis in 1982, is that correct?"

"Yes."

"That would be about the same year you were born, right?"

"Right."

"What kind of marks do you get in history, Mike?"

"What's that got to do with it?"

"I've got to rule out … "

"You think I'm a nut."

"I didn't say that. But I've got to be sure this information you're giving me is unbiased."

"My marks are not a problem."

"Do you like Mr. Dorfman? Is he a good teacher?"

"I don't think my opinion of the murderer has anything to do with it. He killed a thirteen-year-old kid and you're asking me if I like him."

"How do you know Mr. Dorfman killed Sarah Francis?"

"Look, Inspector, let me ask you a question. This isn't 1982, it's 2000. Do you have any of the killer's DNA — from hairs or other personal stuff like blood, saliva, skin maybe — taken from the crime scene? Because if you've got anything at all then all you need is a sample of Dorfman's DNA, and I guarantee it'll be a perfect match. That would be enough to convict him, wouldn't it?"

Samson ran his hands through his bushy hair, his eyes not weary now but questioning and alert. "Usually, yes. But to obtain a sample of your teacher's DNA we'd need either his voluntary cooperation or a warrant. And to obtain either we'd need some evidence that he might have committed the crime. The word of a high school kid just doesn't make it, I'm afraid. There's got to be a distinct possibility your Mr. Dorfman might have done it. You follow me? In other words: no hard evidence, no warrant."

"Sarah Francis was on her way home from debating practice. That much I do know. It was late. Dorfman was the debating coach. He might've given her a lift and then tried to kiss or fondle her in his car. Maybe she didn't like what he was doing and managed to get out of the car and run away and he ran after her to stop her screaming, and maybe he didn't mean to kill her — look, I don't pretend to know exactly *how* it happened, but he did it; that much I know for certain."

"I'm afraid it's no good. That's guesswork, not evidence. So back to my original question: How do you know for certain — as you put it — that Dorfman murdered Sarah Francis?"

"You wouldn't believe me."

"Try me."

"She told me."

"Who told you?"

"Sarah Francis."

"Sarah Francis told you that Dorfman murdered her."

"That's it."

"In 1982."

"Right."

"She told you when you were, what...?" He glanced at his notes. "... a five-month-old baby."

"She didn't tell me in 1982; she told me yesterday."

"Yesterday." Voice flat and suddenly tired.

"Right."

"Seventeen years after she died."

"That's right. I said you wouldn't believe me."

Samson's eyebrows rose in mild astonishment.

"She was, what — a spirit, a ghost? Something like that?"

"I don't know much about spirits or ghosts, Inspector. But she was definitely Sarah Francis."

"A real flesh-and-blood human being."

"That's right. I can tell you what she was wearing when she was murdered. I've checked the newspaper stories. The reports made no mention of what she had on, and there was no way I could've been there, so how would I know, right, Inspector?"

The detective said nothing. His black eyes glittered shrewdly at Mike as he waited for him to continue.

Mike could feel his heart pounding. "Her clothes and everything were muddy. And there was blood. She was wearing a red nylon ski jacket, and it was ripped in the back, a long tear, and her dress was torn, too, and she had only one shoe, a Nike runner."

Inspector Samson glanced through the file. "What color was the dress?"

"Blue. It was a light blue ... with white buttons down the front, most of them torn off and the dress was ripped ... and I bet a blue denim tote bag was found at the scene ..."

"How long you been in the wheelchair?"

Mike could feel himself flushing. "What's that got to do with anything?"

Samson smiled apologetically. "I'll switch off the tape, okay? But I need to know a few things about you, Mike. Put yourself in my place; you're a detective, okay... ?" He leaned over and switched off the tape recorder. "And a seventeen-year-old high school kid comes in and tells you he knows who murdered a girl in 1982, the same year he was born. How does he know? Why, the murdered girl told him, that's how. This seventeen-year-old kid is in a wheelchair because he's lost his legs; looks like he might've had a rough time of it. Life can't be easy for a kid in a wheelchair, who looks around him and sees other kids walking and running, snowboarding, hitting the ski slopes, mountain-biking, going out with girls — you know, regular stuff — so, wouldn't you want to ask the kid about how he feels? About his teacher — who he says is a murderer — and about his girlfriend, if he's got one? And about his family, and how he got to be in a wheelchair? How else you gonna know whether he's telling the truth? You with me, Mike?"

Mike gave a sigh and relaxed. Samson was okay. He was only doing his job.

When he finally got outside, the Lincoln was parked in the handicap slot and Chris was climbing into his wheelchair. "I was just coming in to get you," said Chris. "You've been in there almost two flaming hours."

30 . . . nightmare

He had his legs back again, but it was in a dream, or a nightmare more like.

Sarah was playing a grand piano up on a stage in a concert hall full of people dressed in their best. Full orchestra. She was playing a concerto. He sat listening to her, watching her long white fingers flying over the keys. Next, inexplicably, she was by his side, running, and he was running with her — no wheelchair — from the street into the same concert hall, as the orchestra tuned up before the concert. Her hair hid the side of her face closest to him, but he knew it was Sarah. He held her hand.

"It's so late," said Sarah, worried.

"Don't worry," he heard himself say. "Our seats are reserved."

The orchestra was still tuning up as they reached their aisle. The piano stood waiting for the soloist to appear on the stage.

"It's along here. You first, Sarah."

She released his hand and they excused themselves as they pushed past faceless patrons until they reached their seats. There was a man sitting in Mike's seat. The man said, "You just made it, Sarah. I've saved you a place right here beside me." It was Dorfman, eyes magnified twice as much as usual and gleaming behind his glasses, wet mouth — like in an *Alien* movie — dripping a viscous saliva onto the seat beside him.

"Run, Sarah, run!" Mike cried, pulling at her arm.

The first pounding piano notes of the concerto sounded as they fled back up the aisle, Dorfman in pursuit. Mike tried to look back to see who was playing the piano, but Dorfman was blocking the view. Dorfman reached out and Sarah screamed.

He woke in a lather of sweat, crying and thrashing about and falling out of bed onto the floor.

31 . . . letum non omnia finit

Chris drove him to St. Augustine's and let Mike out at the lich-gate. It was early evening, cold and raw, with a wind that moaned in the church eaves and tossed the bare branches of the graveyard trees.

"I'd rather go alone," said Mike.

"Looks pretty spooky to me. You sure you'll be okay in there?"

"I'll be fine."

"If you're not back in ten minutes, I'll come looking for you."

The graveyard was well cared for, with paved pathways. There was nobody else about, nobody to observe him, which was the way he wanted it.

Most of the graves were very old, their granite slabs cracked and eroded by wind and rain. Many were blackened or clothed in a patina of mossy green. He searched for a fairly new one, a grave only seventeen years old.

He soon found it, a neglected little plot tucked away at the back behind the church, with an unweathered stone. He left the paved path and struggled to push his chair over the wet grass.

Breathing heavily from the effort, he stopped his chair in front of the polished granite grave marker, beside which, fallen onto its side, was an empty, discolored glass jar that had once held flowers.

He could not read the inscription on the grave-stone. He struggled to move his chair in closer.

SARAH STEPHANIE FRANCIS
b. July 14 1969
d. Dec 17 1982

That was all it said. Nothing else.

He didn't know why, but he wanted to take a look at the back of the stone. He pushed himself around, grunting with the effort.

Engraved in the granite were four words:

LETUMNONOMNIAFINIT

It was Latin, he knew that much. *Non* probably meant none or not; *omnia* was all and *finit* probably meant finish or end. But he was guessing. He had no idea of the meaning of *letum*. He read the inscription over several times, memorizing it, then he bowed his head in a brief prayer.

He righted the toppled jar before he left.

With the help of Norma's Latin-English dictionary he translated the grave inscription that same evening.

LETUMNONOMNIAFINIT
NOTALLENDSWITHDEATH

He started reading the book Norma had given him for Christmas. The title of the book was *Fight for the Sky*. It was an autobiography of Squadron Leader Douglas Bader, a W.W. II air ace who flew Spitfires and Hurricanes. Douglas Bader had no legs.

32 . . . all that lives must die

She came at the end of February.

Robbie pushed Mike through the wind and rain
to the Granville Island Market after school and Mike
asked to be left there. He felt restless, didn't want
to go home yet, wanted to sit alone for a while out
on the deck with the huddled pigeons, away from
the shoppers and the lights and the warmth. He felt
a need for turbulence: the wind whipping his hair,
the sight of the churning sea.

Robbie said, "You can't stay out here in this
storm."

"There's a sweater under my raincoat. I'll be
okay."

Robbie left him alone.

He sat facing the far shore of English Bay with
the wind tearing at him, watching the boats in the
marina roll and pitch. Rain lashed his face. He sat
for a long time, ignoring the cold creeping into him.
The wilder the weather became the calmer he felt.
And then he became aware of her presence: he
could feel her near.

An overhead light came on, a dull yellow smudge.

She appeared out of the rain, smiling and happy. "Michael!"

For a moment he hardly recognized her, then his heart lifted. "Sarah!"

She laughed and threw her arms about him. "Oh, Michael!"

The same laugh, the same voice, the same, yet not the same. She was taller, more lovely than ever in a raincoat, green or gray — it was impossible to tell under the yellow light — its collar turned up against the wind and rain. She had no hat or gloves, but a scarf fluttered at her neck.

"You're so grown up, Sarah."

Her hair blew about her face. She held out both her hands and he held them and they stared at each other, smiling and happy, saying nothing, words unnecessary.

Then she pushed his wheelchair through the market and on to the sea wall, where the lights from the upscale waterfront condos shone out at them.

"I can push myself from here," he said. "Walk beside me. I want to look at you." She walked beside him, her hand softly intimate at the back of his neck.

They moved in silence. He had to push harder on the right wheel because of the cambered pavement. He wanted to tell her about the sweat-soaked nightmares he'd been having about Dorfman pursuing her. He wanted to tell her about the police detective, how he kept dropping in to the co-op to ask more questions, how Norma was starting to believe that the accident and the loss of his family was making Mike see things that were not there, and about how ... But he said nothing; those were the wrong words: they would spoil everything.

She was wearing stockings and leather shoes with flat heels. He had never noticed before ... "You're pigeon-toed!"

She laughed. "Isn't it awful? My mother is pigeon-toed too; I get it from her."

He couldn't stop looking at her. She was so grown up. "Let's stop and you can sit on that bench. It's sheltered from the wind here."

"No, Michael. You're cold. You should get home."

"I want to look at you on my level; you're so tall I'm getting a crick in my neck. I can't see your face."

She sat on the edge of the bench. "I don't need to see your face, Michael; I have memorized every line of it."

"Yours has changed, Sarah."

"Yours is changed too."

"Mine? How's that?"

"You used to be such a grouch, hating everyone, frowning, barking at me for no reason — and at everyone else, but now your face is ... happy."

"Because of you."

She pulled her coat around her. The yellow light from the living room of a nearby condo fell on her shoulders and hair, and they sat together in happy silence, isolated in a cocoon of wind and rain, cut off from the world.

Sarah nodded towards the lighted window, whispering. "It looks so warm and peaceful in there. Do you see the woman reading? In an easy chair? The furniture is red and brown and rich. There are paintings on the walls."

He said, "A man is bringing a tray. Tea or coffee. The husband."

"It's tea. I see the teapot. He's asking her something."

"Normal people living normal lives."

"Yes."

He thought about his family and about the people who died every day in airplanes and floods and other disasters. "Why do normal people living normal lives have to die too soon, Sarah?"

"Everything must die; you know that, Michael: leaves, flowers, trees, people, all that lives must die. Some lives are long, others short. It's natural."

"Yeah, but why young people — kids? It doesn't seem right."

The only reply was the squeeze of her hand.

They watched the storm in silence, holding hands. The wind blew Sarah's hair. The front of her coat fell open at the knees revealing a plaid skirt.

Mike said, "Dorfman — "

"Don't say anything, please."

"He ... the police — "

"I know. Say no more. I can read it in your eyes. You are fighting for me." She removed the scarf from her neck. It was red, he could see that now. "You are my brave knight, Michael." She tied the bright scarf to his wheelchair. "You must carry your lady's favor with you into battle."

Then she stood. "You're cold. Your hands are

freezing. And I must go."

"Stay a while longer, Sarah."

"I must go."

"Another minute."

"Wait for me, Michael."

She touched his face with her fingers, lingering. Then she hurried away along the sea wall into the rain, stopping once to look back and wave before she disappeared into the dark.

He sat for a while, watching the place where she had disappeared. Then he ran his fingers through the scarf. Silk. He thought of Sarah's watercolor painting: wheelchair shape, dark head over a red heart, a boy with no legs.

Now he had two things belonging to her.

He wheeled himself home through Bucketwheel Alley.

33 . . . one last look

It was the second semester, and he had four new courses; he was finished with the archives room; his history of Carleton was done. And he was finished with history from Dorfman. The project had earned a good mark, but now it was all over and he need never look at Dorfman's ugly face again.

He made a final visit to his archives room, to tidy up, to take one last look, to sit for a while and think of Sarah and their time there together. He looked around. There were still cobwebs and dirt on the window and in the spaces above the bookshelves and under the sink, but the yearbooks and newspapers were now neatly organized and arranged on the shelves with labels to show the dates. Sarah's work mostly. Then he noticed what looked like a painting on Sarah's side of the desk. He reached over and picked it up. It was a picture of a thin, smiling boy with cropped hair, wearing a white undershirt and dark shorts that covered his knees. It was Charlie Johnson, the high-jumper from False Creek Flats. Sarah had painted him standing in front of a squatter's shack. Mike studied the painting, wondering how many other times Sarah had visited the room when he was not there. He inserted her painting carefully between the pages of his *History of Flight* to take away with him. Then he took one last look around, locked the door and hung the key in Miss Pringle's office.

He wheeled by Dorfman's classroom each morning, impatient to see if the police had taken him away. But no, he was still there, setting up his overhead projector to torture a new set of students. Mike tried to think of a way to convince the police that Dorfman was a murderer. But he could think only of DNA, which was as good as a fingerprint. The technology hadn't been available back in 1982. But now it was. But Detective Samson didn't seem to be doing anything about it. Perhaps he had decided to drop the case. Because it was too unbelievable, too bizarre.

But what if he were to get something of Dorfman's, a hair or two perhaps, and hand them over to Samson? Dorfman usually hung his sports jacket on the back of his chair in the classroom. There were sure to be a few hairs on it; the man was bald on the top of his head, but there was enough hair left around his ears and in his comb-over; balding men shed hairs easily, didn't they?

So that was what he did, that same day, between classes while Dorfman was taking care of his nicotine habit. He wheeled in to the murderer's deserted classroom, picked off three hairs from his jacket and placed them carefully into an envelope, which he sealed and anchored between the covers of his *History of Flight* book in his packsack.

That evening he called Samson and told him he had some physical evidence for him, three hairs in an envelope. Samson told him that it wasn't legal and that he couldn't possibly use them.

A detective arrived twenty minutes later to pick up the envelope.

34 . . . the dark color of his skin

He was tall and athletic and was on the track and soccer teams. He was also on the school's debating team. His name was Ben Packard.

"Hi, I'm Mike Scott and I just wanted to apologize for the way I was earlier this year." They were in the school cafeteria.

Packard frowned. "I offered to get you a Coke. How could I forget? You were pretty unfriendly."

"I was worse: I acted like a real jerk."

"Right on. I figured you for a racist. But I found out later you treat everyone the same — black *and* white, so I didn't feel discriminated against." He grinned, his teeth a shining white against the dark color of his skin.

Mike said, "Let me get you a Coke, okay?"

Packard smiled. "Sure. But make it a grapefruit juice."

The short rainy days of February were all darkness and gloom, but not for Mike, for he felt good. The world around him had taken on a new reality, as if he hadn't ever seen things as they really were before. Colors seemed brighter and sharper; small everyday things, like the bare wet branches of maple trees along the sea wall, seemed important somehow, as if there was something there waiting to be discovered if only he looked hard enough. Silent and still, he watched a glistening black winter twig with its translucent drop of rain and thought of Sarah.

35 . . . forgotten by everyone

Weeks went by. Sarah did not come.

Chris drove Mike to St. Augustine's graveyard one evening with daffodils and a bottle filled with water. Mike filled the glass jar on Sarah's grave with water and flowers.

March battered its way in with bitterly cold gales that downed many trees all over the Lower Mainland. Mike struggled to school against powerful headwinds. Dorfman, child killer, monster, was still in his classroom. Mike pestered Samson's office, trying to get an update on the investigation; the detective inspector was out came the unvarying reply.

Though Norma asked him no further questions about Sarah, Mike could see that she was still worried about his mental health. Even Robbie had stopped asking about Sarah. It was as if Sarah no longer existed: she was gone and forgotten by everyone.

Everyone except Mike.

36 . . . complete and utter silence

"What's with the red scarf?" asked Robbie one Wednesday afternoon as they trundled home.

"It's Sarah's."

"You haven't mentioned her in a while."

"Only because you don't really believe there is a Sarah. You and Norma. Both of you think I made her up. Because I lost my legs. Because I lost my family. Because I lost my mind. You think I imagined it, like it's a movie."

"You're wrong. I believe you, Mike."

"Oh, yeah?"

"I've been doing a lot of thinking and I believe you. I believe you because I know you haven't lost your mind. You're the same guy I've always known. We been pals since we were kids, right? You always stuck up for me, man, especially in elementary school when the other kids were calling me Fatso and all those other names. I know you, Mike. Right now, ever since you met this girl, you're more like your old self, the way you used to be before the accident, not blaming and not mad at everyone.

The other kids at school say you're easier to get along with. You know what I'm saying? I believe you're okay and I believe Sarah's a real girl, because she's the one who did it."

"You really believe me!"

"Yeah. I do."

"But what if I told you she died over seventeen years ago? Would you still believe?"

"Come again?" Robbie stopped the chair and walked around to the front to look his friend in the eye.

"Sarah Francis was murdered back in 1982, Robbie."

"You're kidding me!"

Mike shook his head.

"You're saying she really *is* a ghost?"

He shook his head again. "She's just simply Sarah. She's real to me. That's all I can say."

"Tell me about the murder part."

"You won't say I'm crazy again?"

"I promise, man. I swear — cross my heart and hope to die, okay?"

Robbie got back behind the chair and pushed. As they rolled along, Mike told him how he'd discovered the report of Sarah's murder in the *Clarion* and how Dorfman was the murderer and how Mike had handed the hairs over to the police and how he'd gone to see Sarah's grave.

Robbie, for once, was astonished into complete and utter silence.

On Saturday evening at Robbie's place Mike showed

his friend the *Clarion* report of Sarah's murder. Robbie asked more questions, getting more and more excited. "What a story!" he said. "But I don't get it. How come the police haven't arrested Dorfman? He's the worst kind of slime."

"Evidence, Robbie. They've got to have enough hard evidence to stand up in court. The police haven't told me, but I think everything depends on DNA. If there's a match from the hairs I gave them the least it can do is give them the power to bring him in for questioning. Then they might get further evidence. Who knows? Maybe he'll confess."

"Yeah! I'd make him confess. I'd have the light shining on his ugly face while I questioned relentlessly, cleverly. I'd have teams asking him the same questions over and over, all through the day and night, never allowing him to sleep, and when he nods off, waking him and starting in again with the questions, pounding away at him until he breaks down and gives a written confession, sobbing onto the paper."

Mike grinned. "You've seen too many of those old black-and-white detective movies, Robbie."

They had watched it before, but they — once again — vegged out in front of *Raiders of the Lost Ark* on video, and ate popcorn. Then they watched Indiana Jones again in *The Last Crusade*.

When the movies were over, they were tired. Robbie said sleepily, "You know what, Mike? That story of yours, it would make a great movie!"

37 . . . a feeling she would come

He had a feeling she would come.

He wheeled down to the sea wall late one evening through a thickening mist coming in from the sea and sat, peering at the faint glow of lights from West End towers across the water and inhaling the pungent smell of seaweed exposed by a low tide. Though there was no wind, mist and dampness made him wish he'd dressed more warmly, a thick sweater instead of the thin jacket.

The mist drifted about the sea wall and the dark trees and the damp benches. The sound of a truck on Cambie Bridge, muted by the mist and damp coastal air, faded away into silence.

He was starting to shiver; he should go back.

The silence was broken suddenly by the high, ringing sound of footsteps hurrying along the sea wall, and then the mist slid and shifted like a door opening as she came running towards him, breathless and happy.

His heart gave a lurch. "Sarah!" His voice suddenly hoarse, his body no longer cold.

She kneeled beside the chair and flung her arms

about him. "Oh, Michael!"

Each time he saw her she was a little different, a little older, a little taller — or so it seemed — and more lovely, more fresh and alive.

They moved to a bench and she sat, clasping his hands, and they stayed like this for several minutes, enjoying the silence and their closeness.

"It is wonderful to see you, Michael. You are so strong and well."

"And you look wonderful, like a movie star, Sarah. Remember how you liked to play those stupid movie star games?"

"You were such a sorehead."

"No, I wasn't."

"Yes, you were."

They laughed.

"You graduate soon, Michael. I want to be there to see it."

"You will come to grad?"

"I will try very hard to be there, Michael. It will be a graduation for me, too."

He didn't understand. Her hands were warm.

He said, "I decided I'm going back to Rehab to get fitted with a pair of tin legs."

"Legs? And then you can walk?"

"That's what they tell me. It will take a couple of months to learn, once they get the legs for me."

"I'm happy for you, Michael. This will be good for you, I know. What made you decide?"

"A book Norma gave me. An English air ace named Douglas Bader lost both his legs, like me, but he was super-determined to fly and he did. He flew fighter planes with his artificial ones. He called them 'tin' legs."

"Your aunt is a smart woman."

"Yes."

"I think you can do it, Michael."

He smiled and shrugged his shoulders. "I can try."

"They're not really tin, are they, these legs?"

"No. Metal and plastic, I think, but I haven't seen them yet. I will need canes or crutches for a while, until I get used to them."

They talked. She stayed until it was very dark and the mist had caused all the lights from the West End towers to disappear. He felt tired and sleepy and barely noticed her hands slip away.

The first week was impossible. If the therapists hadn't continued to encourage him every time he lost his balance and fell he would have quit by the end of it.

Adjustments were made to the legs.

The second week was also bad: he wanted to give up. The muscles in his thighs ached with weariness and his stumps were irritated and sore. "We've got to build the muscles up," they said. "Exercise is the answer." He exercised at Rehab and he exercised at home.

Further adjustments were made to the legs and to the socks and the cushioning.

By the end of the third week he was beginning to get the hang of it; he fell less often and could walk a short distance without the aid of canes. "The more you practice the better you will become," they said. "Practice, practice."

He continued to use his wheelchair: it would be

a long time yet before he would be ready to walk in public.

38 . . . charged with murder

"It made the *Vancouver Sun*," said Robbie. "Look! It even made the *Globe and Mail*." He dropped the newspapers on Norma's kitchen table and pulled up a chair. Mike picked up the *Sun*. The front page showed a picture of masked federal agents with guns, breaking into a Miami home to snatch the six-year-old Cuban boy, five months after he had been pulled from the sea.

"Not that story, stupid," said Robbie. He turned the page.

Mike stared at a picture of Dorfman — taken when he had hair — with the caption, "Albert Dorfman in 1982." The headline read: "TEACHER CHARGED WITH MURDER."

"They got him!" cried Mike. "They got Dorfman!"

There was also a picture of Dorfman's arrest: flanked by three plainclothes officers, he was being led, handcuffed, to a waiting police car.

"Everything you told me was true," said Robbie, excited.

Mike stared at his friend. "You didn't believe me?"

Robbie flushed with embarrassment. "Of course I believed you. I just wasn't sure about the Dorfman part. He's slime, I knew that, but I wasn't so sure about a Carleton teacher as a killer, that's all. Teachers are the good guys, right? If it was a movie it would be the janitor."

"And you call yourself a pal!"

"Look, man, I'll never doubt anything you tell me ever again, I promise, okay? I swear. If you tell me Air Canada needs you to test a new supersonic jet, I'll believe you, honest!"

Sarah didn't come again that month. She didn't come again until June. Until grad day.

She came to see him graduate.

35 . . . graduation

"Lillian Fonzatelli," called Miss Pringle in her best black dress. Miss Pringle always read out the names at graduation; it was a tradition.

"Arthur Samuel Forbes," called Miss Pringle.

The ceremony at Carleton High was formal, with the boys in suits and ties, the girls in white dresses or gowns, all seated in the gymnasium in more-or-less alphabetical order. The gymnasium was decorated with flowers and banners. Parents and other relatives sat up in the balcony. The grads sat in the auditorium, girls on one side, boys on the other, rising and walking forward to the stage as their names were called.

Mike sat in his wheelchair, not ready yet to show off his new legs.

Then Sarah was there, suddenly, standing beside him, in a white gown that contrasted with her shining dark hair. She looked lovely. He looked up at her and she smiled and placed a hand on his shoulder and he understood what she had meant about this day being graduation for her too.

He waited for his name to come up, excited, thinking, not of himself, but of Sarah when she was a kid, how he'd almost run over her feet with his wheelchair that first time. And now she was grown up, no longer a little kid. Sarah Stephanie Francis. She had never mentioned that middle name, the one on her grave. There was still so much he didn't know about her, had never heard her play the piano, had never …

"Robert Brent Palladin," called Miss Pringle.

Mike tore his eyes away from Sarah as Robbie bounced up onto the stage for his diploma and handshake, self-conscious in his new suit. Then he thumped back down the stairs, his face creased in a huge smile, brandishing his "Dogwood," British Columbia's flower symbol, certificate like a sword.

Soon it was Mike's turn.

"Michael Scott," called Miss Pringle.

He didn't want to leave her, but he had to go. "Wait for me, Sarah."

They had provided a ramp for him. He wheeled onto the stage and received his Dogwood. As he shook hands with the principal he could see his aunt up in the balcony, waving her program wildly. He searched frantically for Sarah. There she was, smiling up at him. He grinned, then shot back down the ramp, showing off his wheelchair skills, back to his spot in the aisle near Robbie.

But Sarah had gone.

When the valedictory address was done and the band and the choir had performed their final number, when the ceremony was over, everyone crowded out of the gym and along the hallway to the cafeteria for pop and pastries. Mike searched amid the confusion of formal dresses and gowns for a sight of Sarah. Boys and girls chattered to each other. He finally made it to the crowded cafeteria where Norma was waiting for him, her eyes bright with tears. She bent and kissed him and hugged his embarrassed face to her plump chest.

When she released him, he said, "I owe you a lot, Norma. I don't know what I would've — "

"Ah, hush," said Norma. "You're more son than nephew, Mike. You know that. I'm owed nothing."

He looked around for Sarah, but she was not there.

40 . . . fast like a fist

He had a job at the Center for July, talking with recently handicapped kids whose dives into rivers had fractured spinal vertebrae, or kids like himself who had survived vehicle accidents. He enjoyed the work. By the end of the first week the counselors were saying that his cheerful, positive attitude was powerful medicine, just what the kids needed as they tried to make difficult adjustments. The pay wasn't much, but it made him feel useful, and it would help Norma pay their bills.

At Rehab he walked on his new legs as much as possible. When he became too tired he used his trusty old wheelchair, which now had rear racks for his legs.

Robbie went to work in a furniture warehouse and was talking about staying on after the summer if a permanent job came up.

Government exam results came through. Mike and Robbie had passed everything. Robbie was so surprised and happy he brought a bottle of British Columbia's best champagne around to Mike's to go with Norma's cheesecake.

"I'm so proud of you both," said Norma, raising

her glass. Dolly Dhaliwal came over for a visit with her husband and two boys and a plate of sticky cakes. The boys were twins. One was called Arshad, the other Varin. Mike couldn't tell them apart. They sat silently together on Norma's loveseat and ate the pastries.

When everyone had gone, Mike went to his room and examined his yearbook's gold cover and inscription: "Carleton High School. 1999-2000." Inside was "Carleton's First Fifty Years," with archival photographs, text by Mike Scott, and a watercolor painting of a boy named Charlie Johnson painted by "sf." He turned to his favorite page, the one amid the pages of "2000 Grads" with its elementary school black-and-white picture — clipped from the *Clarion* and pasted in by Mike — of Sarah Stephanie Francis, the girl whose graduation came eighteen years late.

He didn't expect to see her again, he didn't know why, except there had been something final in the way she'd been there at his graduation, and the way she had looked at him. He could practically swear that the shine in her eyes had been tears. What had she said on the sea wall? It was a graduation for her, too? Then she was gone. It was all over. Dorfman's criminal trial would be coming up in October and then it would all be over for sure. He felt once more that crushing sense of loss, that emptiness in his life, which couldn't be filled. But he had to try anyway, concentrating on work at the Center, concentrating on walking practice, keeping himself busy, keeping himself useful.

At the end of the third week he was so tired he had hardly enough energy to swing himself up out

of his chair and onto his bed. Norma wasn't home
yet. He closed his eyes. Sounds of her radio drifted
in his open door. Damn! He should have switched it
off. He made a move towards the door but then
stopped, listening.

*... Air France Concorde crashed ... only a
minute after taking off from Paris ... bound for New
York ... German passengers ... everyone killed ...
total of 113 people.*

He strained to hear more, but the news item was
finished.

A supersonic Concorde! The Concorde was beautiful. They never crashed; everyone knew that. The
deaths. A hundred and thirteen. People in suits and
dresses and stockings and shoes, with rings and hand-
bags and laptops and wristwatches, all killed. What
had they been thinking about as the plane was taking off? Were they looking forward to seeing Man-
hattan from the top of the World Trade Center or the
Empire State Building? Or were they thinking of stocks
and bonds and planning for their old age pensions
many years in the future? Not knowing they would be
dead in less than one minute.

Death coming fast like a fist.

He closed his eyes again, hearing the buzz of
the radio, seeing Becky and his parents ... and Sarah.

Soon he was asleep, flying in the clouds, his hands
on the controls of his Spitfire, the confident scream
of the plane's Merlin engine in his ears, the smell of
leather and oil in his nostrils, the sight of the bril-
liant high blue as he burst up out of the clouds
towards the sun.

41 . . . leave me alone

David Barnwell was new at the Center. He had lost a leg, amputated below the knee, in a motorcycle accident. He was sixteen years old.

David reminded Mike of himself, how he used to be when he was first sent to the Center. David yelled at everyone, refused to practice with crutches, refused to eat, messed his bed, wouldn't even look at the temporary wheelchair they were trying to get him to use. His parents visited, trying their best to reason with him, but he stared ahead, arms folded, saying nothing, waiting for them to go and leave him alone. His chart was marked: *Diffic.*

"Welcome to Heartbreak Hotel," Mike said as he wheeled into the room at their first meeting. There was no response. Mike tried to talk with the boy, but David was having none of it. He covered his head with a blanket, refusing to listen. "Leave him," the nurses advised. "Try again in a day or two."

But David's behavior didn't improve. A week went by, and then another. Finally, Mike talked to the boy through his protective blanket. "You can't cover yourself up forever, David."

"Drop dead," came the muffled reply.

"I used to be like you, David. In this place. Mad at everyone. Mad at the world. I think I can help. But you've got to let me try."

"Leave me alone!"

"David?"

"Drop dead!"

"You've got to talk to me."

"Talk to the well-behaved crippled robot in his wheelchair?" he yelled from under his blanket. "So I can be a good little crippled robot too, like you, and have all these stupid fat pop-eyed jerks who call themselves doctors and nurses pat me on the head for being a good boy and doing as I'm told? You gotta be kidding me!"

"Wheelchair? What wheelchair?"

The covers moved. David peeped out, scowling. Blue eyes clouded with grief, brown hair long and wild. "Mind your own stupid business and leave me al — " He stared at Mike, standing beside his bed without aid, hands on hips. David's disbelieving eyes moved down to Mike's new legs.

Mike walked closer to the bed.

He said, "I used to be a runner. I was on the track team. But that was then and this is now. I got over it. How do you like my new tin legs? Pretty good, huh?"

David's mouth hung open; he was speechless.

"You've still got one good leg left. And most of your other leg. You're lucky. You can walk with the help of crutches, then later with a tin leg like mine. It's called a prosthesis. You won't have to push a wheelchair around and look up to everyone like you're a six-year-old kid the rest of your life; you'll be able to walk again, run, ski even. You hear what I'm saying?"

The boy looked at him for the longest time, and then he said, "What did you say your name was?"

"Mike."

"I'll be able to ski?"

"I don't see why not. Or snowboard. Whatever."

David stared at him.

Mike said, "I gotta go."

"You want to pass me some juice?" He pointed to the table at the end of the bed.

Mike moved a few steps and passed the juice.

"You coming tomorrow?"

"You going to start listening to the nurses?"

"They can all drop dead."

Mike turned and walked towards the door.

"Mike?"

He stopped and turned.

"I'll think about it."

Mike left, grinning to himself.

As the weeks went by, the need for his services at the Center increased substantially: he was now a permanent member of the team. He had a proper job and a title: Youth Director. His small salary increased as he learned to take on extra responsibilities. His effect on patients was therapeutic. He chatted with accident victims in their rooms, helping to ease them out of depression, boosting their morale, providing comfort. He brought them books from the Center's library, and wrote letters or filled out forms if they were unable to do so for themselves.

He and Norma drove to his family's graves at Forest Lawn a couple of times a month, and every week he drove himself in Chris's car to Sarah's grave, to tidy and leave flowers. He always left a message under the glass jar for her to read.

Norma was delighted with the change in him. "It's wonderful to see you fit and happy, Mike. Joanne would be proud of you, and your father too."

He made himself believe it, that his father would be proud of him.

He was able to walk long stretches of the sea wall, and continued his outings with Robbie to Granville Island or to the Maritime Museum whenever they could get together. They pushed the empty wheelchair, though Mike was depending on it less and less as his skill and stamina increased. Robbie, for his part, was not only slimmer and gaining extra muscle in his arms and shoulders, but he also had more confidence in himself. The warehouse was only the beginning, he explained to Mike; he was learning the furniture business from the bottom up. He aimed to get into the import end of the industry and maybe start his own business someday.

Robbie really would start his own business someday; Mike believed that. When he set his mind on something, he always followed through.

"You'll be famous, Robbie," said Mike. "I can see it now: Robbie Palladin, well-known tycoon and billionaire, renowned film producer, creator of *Casablanca 2* and other fine movies."

"Now there's an idea," Robbie said, grinning. "Nobody's ever done another *Casablanca*."

42 . . . once and for all

There was a birthday cake for Mike at the Center.

It had his name on the top in bright red icing. He was surprised. Everyone had come to the cafeteria: the nurses and therapists, the resident physician Dr. Ryan, the patients, even the nurses and aides from the night shift. He blew out the candles and everyone sang, "Happy birthday." The senior nurse, Marion Chadwick, made a speech, thanking him for the fine work he was doing for the Center, and presented him with flowers and a gift certificate amid cheers and applause. Mike felt himself blush a deeper, hotter red than that of the cake icing.

Later, at home, he picked up his father's photograph and pretended it was speaking to him: "Fine work, Michael. Well done, son. Way to go!"

He waited impatiently for the trial to begin, to prove Dorfman's guilt once and for all.

His name was Greg Stevenson and he flew a two-place ultralight. His partner had failed to turn up for a day's flying, so when he saw Mike standing, watching the fliers through a pair of binoculars, he strolled over.

"You're usually in a wheelchair, ain't that right? I've seen you here lots of times."

"That's right," said Mike.

"You're walking now. Great!"

Mike grinned self-consciously and demonstrated by walking back and forth a few paces.

"This is my aunt, Norma McLeod, and my friend Robbie."

"Hi. Greg Stevenson. Pleased to meet you." He stuck out his hand. Then he turned back to Mike. "You ever fly in one of these?" He jerked his head at his ultralight.

Mike knew it was a Beaver RX 550 Plus. Greg's was red, with what looked like a big Rotax engine, a 582 maybe. "Never," he said. He didn't like to mention he'd never been up in a plane, period.

"I was wonderin' if you might like to take a short spin?"

Mike looked at his aunt. She shrugged and smiled.

"I'd like that," said Mike, trying to hide his excitement.

"I can find you somethin' warm. Make sure you don't freeze to death."

He followed Greg over to the aircraft, pulled on a flying suit and climbed, with help, into the back seat, his heart pounding with anticipation and excitement.

And he flew. For the first time in his life he flew. It was as simple and wonderful as that.

It was time. A thick fog crouched over False Creek. The city was muffled in gloom. They took the small twelve-passenger Aquabus ferry over to an invisible Beach Avenue, and Robbie pushed Mike uphill — the journey was too much of a challenge for his tin legs — along Howe Street through half-blind traffic. They were dressed warmly; Mike and Robbie wore their baseball caps, Norma a toque and walking shoes and she carried her umbrella.

The fog was thinner in the downtown, at the crest of the hill. They were early, so they walked to Robson Square to watch a peaceful demonstration in progress — about a hundred people — outside the art gallery, with signs and billboards protesting what they believed to be the Algerian government's complicity and cover-up of one hundred thousand murders. And across the street an old man paced up and down, carrying a sign above his head: THE END IS NEAR. The traffic was noisy.

The courtroom was crowded, but Detective Inspector Samson was there and he made space for them near the front. Mr. Dorfman sat at a table with his back to the court; all Mike could see of him was the back of his head.

They were there all day, listening to the evidence.

There were no demonstrators in the square on the second day except for the old man shuffling up and down outside the courthouse with his sign: THE END IS NEAR.

On the third day the fog was thicker, and the old man with the sign wasn't there.

On the sixth day Mike, Robbie and Norma sat where they could see Dorfman more clearly. He looked wooden, impassive. The case wound down.

On the ninth day the judge instructed the jury and they retired to consider their verdict.

On the tenth day the fog had gone and the old man with the sign was back and the jury reached its verdict: "Albert Dorfman, guilty of murder in the first degree."

Mike could see Dorfman's face as the jury foreman read the verdict. Dorfman showed no emotion. Dark blue suit, blue shirt, red tie, wet lips, bald head, pale eyes. Nor did he show emotion as Judge John B. Watterson sentenced him to life imprisonment with no chance of parole.

43 . . . one last time

Because it was a busy summer for Mike and Robbie they saw less of each other. When they did get together they had much to talk about, Robbie with stories of the furniture warehouse and the people who worked there, and Mike with his tales of the Rehab Center.

Norma spent her two weeks summer holiday simply relaxing around the apartment, visiting with neighbors, reading, listening to the radio, watching the TV in the evenings as she surfed the channels, hunting for political news, gossip and disaster stories, and talking to her friends in the co-op about August's global tragedies: forest wildfires, the worst in fifty years; a terrorist bomb killing eight in a Moscow subway tunnel close to the Kremlin; Basque separatists killing more innocent people with car bombs; the tragic deaths of 118 men in *Kursk*, their Russian submarine. Norma had lots to talk about.

Dolly Dhaliwal came over one evening with her box of tricks and gave Norma the full treatment over herb tea and sticky cakes.

Mike had tea and cake and asked Dolly to read his palm. She told him he would suffer a loss, and this time he believed her.

Then suddenly it was the end of September and the summer was over.

He was wrong when he'd guessed he would never see Sarah again, for she came on a foggy October evening when the False Creek sea wall was cold and deserted. After a full day at the Center he walked the short distance to Stamps Landing through the fog and watched the ghostly shapes of ships moving up the creek towards Granville Bridge. He listened, but could hear nothing. Vancouver was muffled, almost silent. The silence was welcome after the noise and bustle of the Rehab Center. He wore dark corduroys over his tin legs, and wore his rain jacket, but no hat. His feet felt wet; he grinned wryly.

He thought about Sarah. He was always thinking about Sarah it seemed. And Becky, of course. He would never forget his sister, or Mom and Dad: they were still a powerful ache in his heart.

His home and his family gone. Sarah gone. But his life had meaning now. He had a job, helping others like himself; and he was walking. He was happy, happier than he had been in a very long time.

Sounds began to filter in: the cry of a gull, the faint slap of water against boat hulls in the marina, the tinkling bells, the fading roar of a bus over the Cambie Bridge. He felt the air sliding and shifting about him, saw the fog swirling and lifting with a rush, and her warm hands were suddenly on his face. The voice came from behind, a calm whisper in his ear. "I'm here, Michael."

"Sarah!"

She moved in front of him. Under a loose gray raincoat she wore a plain gray dress that matched her eyes, her grayness merging with the fog. He blinked his eyes to be sure she was really there.

It was Sarah all right, the same Sarah, but with a different aura about her, not smiling as usual, but with a sadness, a kind of still quietness that made her seem almost a stranger.

"Michael, my brave knight. I am so happy to see you. And look at you! Standing tall. I'm proud of you."

He felt his throat tighten. "It feels good to stand. And to look at you."

"Your tin legs."

The fog swirled about them.

"After grad, I didn't think I would ever see you again, Sarah. It was … a feeling. And then I thought, No. She will come to say goodbye."

She turned her head away and looked towards the city lights, barely visible through the fog.

"It's true isn't it? You've come to say goodbye."

She turned back to him, her eyes suddenly bright with tears. "Not goodbye, Michael." She took his hands in hers. "Goodbye is forever."

"So I will see you again?"

"Not for a very long time. But you kept your promise. You waited. Now it's my turn."

He wanted to ask her what she meant, but he couldn't speak. All he knew was that he didn't want her to leave. They walked a short distance, holding hands, and sat together on a bench.

"I miss you, Sarah. And I miss the archives room and our talks. I keep remembering when you were just an eighth grade kid, only months ago, yet a hundred years seem to have passed since then."

"Yes. I came to help you."

"You have helped me more than I can ever say."

"You called me a nuisance."

"No, I didn't."

She smiled. "Yes, you did."

"Didn't."

"You said I smelled like a bubble-gum factory ..."

"And I smelled like ... what was it?"

"A pepperoni pizza." She laughed. "You were such an old sourpuss. Do you remember I said you looked like Harrison Ford, that same scowl? You still look like him, you know; those eyes. And those hurt lines in your face. But you're happy now; your life is good."

"Yes."

She whispered, "I'm leaving you now, Michael." She pulled away, but he held on to her hands, not letting her go.

"What will happen to you, Sarah? Where will you — ?"

She placed a finger on his lips.

The rain splattered in the puddles. The faint glow of light from apartments and high office towers across the inlet twinkled through the mist. The mournful cry of the Prospect Point foghorn came up the inlet. He could feel the weight of the fog on his shoulders.

He released her hands and hugged her. She was solid in his arms, and warm.

After a while she freed herself and backed away from him, and when she was far away, waved; and he tried to wave back but his arms suddenly had no life in them. When she was so far away that he could barely see her face she waved one last time, and then she merged with the gray landscape and the swirling mist. The sea wall was empty. For a long time he stood, staring into the darkness at the spot where she had disappeared. Then he walked back along the sea wall and headed for home.